Alun Lewis (1915-1944) was one of the generation of writers born in the first two decades of the twentieth century who contributed significantly to Welsh literature in English. Born in Cwmaman, near Aberdare, he attended Cowbridge Grammar School and studied history at University College, Aberystwyth, from 1932. His poems and stories appeared in school and college magazines during those early years. After an M.A. at Manchester in 1935 and a year teacher training in Aberystwyth, he joined the staff of the Lewis School, Pengam, before enlisting in the Royal Engineers in May, 1940.

In 1941, he married Gweno Ellis, whom he had met three years before. After attending an Officers' Training course in Morecambe, he joined the Sixth Battalion, the South Wales Borderers as Second Lieutenant and sailed to India in October, 1942. His first volume, *Raiders' Dawn and other poems*, appeared earlier that year and was followed by *The Last Inspection [and other stories]* in 1943. A second volume of poems, prepared in India, appeared after his death in 1945 as *Ha! Ha! Among the Trumpets. In the Green Tree*, including extracts from his letters to his wife and parents and some late stories, was published in 1948.

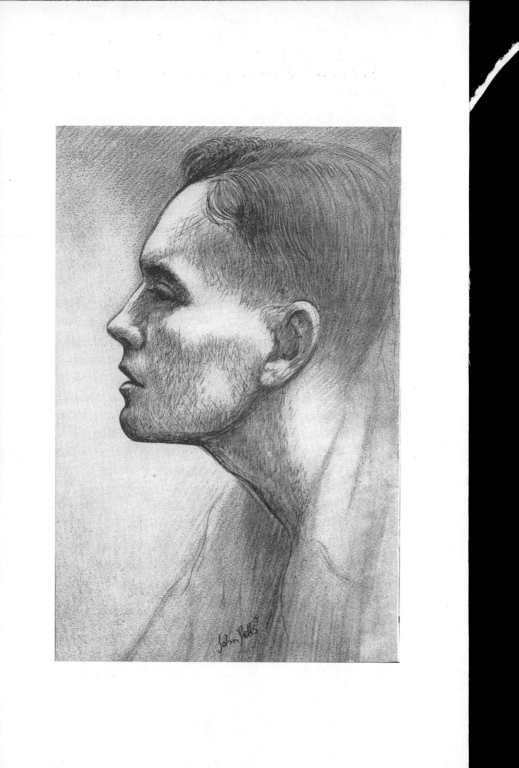

IN THE GREEN TREE

ALUN LEWIS

DRAWINGS BY JOHN PETTS

PARTHIAN
LIBRARY OF WALES

Parthian
The Old Surgery
Napier Street
Cardigan
SA43 1ED
www.parthianbooks.co.uk

The Library of Wales is a Welsh Assembly Government initiative
which highlights and celebrates Wales' literary heritage in the
English language.

The publisher acknowledges the financial support of the Welsh
Books Council.

The Library of Wales publishing project is based at
Trinity College, Carmarthen, SA31 3EP.
www.libraryofwales.org

Series Editor: Dai Smith

First published in 1948
© Gweno Lewis 1948
Library of Wales edition published 2006
Revised edition John Pikoulis
Foreword © Owen Sheers
Afterword © John Pikoulis
All Rights Reserved

ISBN 1902638875
     9781902638874

Cover image courtesy of photolibrary.com
Cover design by Marc Jennings
Illustrations by John Petts

Printed and bound by Gwasg Gomer, Llandysul, Wales
Typeset by logodædaly

British Library Cataloguing in Publication Data

A cataloguing record for this book is available from the British
Library.

Sonnet on
the death of Alun Lewis

Vernon Watkins

He was astonished by the abundance of gold
Light. In the street a beggar stretched her hand,
Dying. Then the shudder ran through him. Once he had planned
To out-distance the sun in a chariot. But how might he hold
That instant, those uncurbed horses, and mix the mould
Her liquid shadow near the lotus and timeless sand?
A slighter man would have noticed the ripples expand
From the stark, regenerate symbol. But to him that cold
Figure was real. Ah yes, he died in the green
Tree. What was it, then, pierced him, keen as a thorn,
And left him inarticulate, humble, unable to scorn
A single soul found on Earth? O, had he seen
In a flash, all India laid like Anthony's queen
Or seen the highest, for which alone we are born?

LIBRARY OF WALES

FOREWORD

Let me begin with a confession. Until I was asked to write the foreword to this new Library of Wales edition of *In the Green Tree*, Alun Lewis was a writer who had only occupied the periphery of my literary vision. Like most, I knew him as a poet. More specifically I knew him as a war poet. I knew he'd died in Burma at the age of just twenty-eight. I knew a handful of his poems and I knew, by heart, the last line of what is probably his best known:

> Where Edward Thomas brooded long
> On death and beauty – til a bullet stopped his song.

So when I opened the cover of a borrowed first edition of *In the Green Tree* it was as a newcomer to Lewis the prose writer. By the time I'd closed the book, I was both delighted and dismayed that this had been the case. Delighted because I'd been able to experience that rarest of literary thrills – the discovery of a voice full of integrity, fresh upon the ear and eye, that speaks to you immediately with an electric vitality. Dismayed because I'd been ignorant of Lewis' uniquely sensitive, young man's old man's voice for so long.

This foreword, then, is written with the enthusiasm of a recent convert – but I hope that may be appropriate as this new edition will attract not just those returning to Lewis' prose, but also those, like me, who will be reading him for the first time.

In the Green Tree is a collection of letters and short stories written between 1943 and 1944, and published in 1948. Long out of print, this republication in the Library of Wales series reproduces that first edition selection. The illustrations by John Petts that originally accompanied the text have been preserved along with the introductory sonnet by Vernon Watkins, a line of which lends the book its title.

In a letter to his wife Gweno in April 1943, Lewis wrote: 'There doesn't seem to be any question more directly relevant than this one of what survives of all the beloved.' Like many of his contemporaries living in the shadow of the war and their own mortality this question was one that welled ever larger in Lewis' mind as the dates of his correspondence crept closer to the morning of his death in March 1944. What will be his legacy? What will he, or any of us, leave behind when we are gone?

Lewis was partly to answer this question through his poetry, both in lines such as, 'But love will survive the venom of the snake', and through the survival of the poems themselves. But what survives of the writer beyond the poems? What, for example, survives of him in this book, in this leaning together of his letters and stories?

One thing is for sure, as John Pikoulis indicates in his afterword: however intimate and unrestrained we might expect personal letters to be, the 'whole' Alun Lewis is far from represented in this selection, which was chosen not by Lewis himself, but by his wife Gweno and the original editor, Gwyn Jones. For all the reasons stated by Pikoulis, another side to Lewis, one that is several shades darker psychologically, has been winnowed from this correspondence to his loved ones back home.

The very fact that Lewis is such a careful, acute writer also pares away what might usually be gleaned from such correspondence – the slips, the rawness, the moments of unguarded emotion or thought. If there's one thing these letters aren't, it's uncrafted. What survives in them of Lewis is, if not the complete man, then certainly a fascinating pattern of the contradictory pressures and sensitivities that made up that man; a pattern revealed through a latticework of shifting concerns and perspectives that build to present not one, but the many versions of Alun Lewis created in the crucible of his wartime situation.

The Lewis of the opening pages is the young Welsh schoolmaster, once a pacifist, now a newly trained officer, travelling far from home, thrown into the 'sprawling gamble of big empires grappling for blood and oil and palm nuts'. As his personal world contracts about him to the restrictive orbit of army routine, so his wider world is simultaneously expanding. 'The world is much larger than just England isn't it?' he writes to Gweno. 'I'll never be just English or just Welsh again.' Upon his sudden entrance into this 'larger' world, however, it is often his connection to Wales and his home-life that anchors and orientates him. Again and again Lewis overcomes the increasing distance between himself and Gweno by evoking their shared temporal, if not physical, space, and more than once he recasts India in the light of his familiar touchstones in Wales, looking for connection in the midst of so much difference.

After his entry into the army in England, Lewis was soon aware that his personality was unsuited to the 'conventional life of the Mess, the officer-mind and its artificial assumptions'. On service in India, the contradictory pressures of Lewis' character and his situation were accentuated and began to play upon him almost immediately. At times he seems remarkably in tune with his new surroundings, when he recreates a scene with the descriptive eye of the talented travel writer, or when he immerses himself in the country's natural world. But such moments of forgetful tranquillity are only ever just that – moments. More often, Lewis is uncomfortable in India. His socialist leanings make it impossible for him to shake off the imperialist underpinnings of his role in the country or to ignore the 'perpetual under-current of hostility among the people' towards the colonial British. 'I wish I had come here as a doctor, teacher, social worker,' he writes to Gweno. 'Anything but a soldier.'

Even when Lewis does feel a connection with the culture and people, his role prevents him from entering its stream entirely. However much he might desire to be 'be away among them and of them', he cannot be, and as the months in India drag past, his desire and ability to 'live one's own part' becomes what he is increasingly anxious to protect.

That 'own part', for Lewis, means writing. Through all of his incarnations in these letters – as officer, traveller, husband, socialist – it is the writer who remains the constant at the centre of his shifting, restless world.

Lewis' prose is limpid, precise and effortlessly alive, but the writer it most often reveals in these letters is Lewis the poet. For me, this is when Lewis' correspondence is at its most interesting, when he turns away from the war and the world to describe instead the interior landscape of his poetic process. This is when, as readers, we are afforded a position of privileged witness on the shoulder of a poet as he moves closer to his finished work.

Lewis seems to find both anguish and exhilaration in this process. At times it embodies an almost physical struggle:

> I was enticed, seduced, and destroyed by the long octopus arms and the hungry hard mouth of a poem that will never be written. It seized me with soft little thrills as I entered the tent, and each night long after midnight I wrestled vainly with it in the long battle of thought and words. When I did at last go to bed I felt spiritually bewildered and unnerved, as though the thoughts had battered and exhausted me.

About the poems and stories that did get written, Lewis may have had the occasional doubt, but nowhere in these letters does he ever seriously question his talent or vocation as a writer. On the contrary, the sincerity and conviction of his intent is one of the most seductive aspects of his voice:

> I feel more and more that my metier *is* writing: that that's the only real thing I can do. I can be a moderately good soldier, but not *very* good...

> Moreover I find my memory, in my 29th year, is taking a new and definite shape to itself. It's discarding everything it doesn't need to write and dream upon.

With such growing confidence in his writing it isn't surprising that Lewis was convinced there was much more still within him, and I've no doubt he was right. But time was not on his side, and so the letters stop. The last paragraph he writes to Gweno begins, 'I must run now. Sorry I have to go.' And four lines later, he has gone.

Where the journey of the letters stops and that of the stories begins provides a fascinating and paradoxical juxta-position: as Lewis moves further away, eclipsed by his own fictional voice, so his concerns and sympathies come closer. The world that has inhabited the background of his letters is suddenly enacted and evoked. Freed from the constraints of the personal, Lewis is able to translate his experiences, desires and thoughts into the voices of his characters.

Lewis himself is of course still present, as are many of the factual roots to these stories, but that's one of the most interesting things about the arrangement of letters and stories in this book: the opportunity to trace the transmutation of lived experience into fiction. The communal farms of British Mandate Palestine that Lewis overhears described by the young Welsh soldier on the troop ship provide the central motif for his masterpiece 'The Orange Grove'. Lewis' wish 'to be away among them and of them', meanwhile, is surely granted when the protagonist of the same story is gradually stripped of his army life before being rescued by a group of gypsies. The 'sort of crisis in your body and mind as you watch events rapidly developing' that Lewis describes during a training exercise informs the tone of 'The Raid' (a worryingly contemporary story when read in the shadow of the Iraq war), while the meeting with his brother Gwyn in Bombay not only provides the setting for 'The Reunion', but also no doubt fuels the bitterness and fear that drives that elliptical narrative.

The stories are assured, mature and resonant. They reveal a writer with a natural ear for speech and a skilled handling of pace, who is capable of the most lambent of lyrical touches without losing focus on the lived and physical world. They are also stories possessed of a subtle psychological depth that moves them far beyond mere narrative description. I often found myself re-reading them almost immediately, and on each reading, discovering more both to admire and to understand.

The new Library of Wales edition of *In the Green Tree* will make possible a wider discovery and retention of Alun Lewis for this century's readers. When you turn this page you'll start your own journey back to wartime India with its author. As you travel, listen to Lewis' voice, to the voices of his fiction, and then listen to the unspoken dialogue between his letters and his stories, made possible by their leaning against each other in this book. Because it's there, in that conversation between his personal and fictional voice, that Alun Lewis survives.

Owen Sheers

IN THE
GREEN TREE

Contents

LETTERS FROM INDIA

THE VOYAGE

1

November, 1942

I've got a little while before I plunge into a sweating hold to see that a piano accordion sing-song is in progress, and then up to the wireless cabin for 'On Board Tonight'. I'm in my hot little cabin and I thought I'd be alone but in come Tudor and another batman called D.O. Evans who is known everywhere as Bugger All Evans! They pretend they've got work to do in our cabin but really it's simply to have somewhere less unbearably sweltering than the crowded hold in which they are forced to exist – what places they are! The bunks piled high to the roof round the hatches and on the hatches, men like maggots playing the old soldiers' gambling game 'Housey-Housey' and the croupier shouting the number in a voice like a bull. Hammocks, beer bottles, oranges, bare legs protruding from shirts, sweat and smell and foetid warmth. And we've only just begun!

PROSPECT OF INDIA

2

November, 1942

I don't know whether to dive in or stay on the bank and concern myself with tanks only. At least I considered both courses, but the insatiable humanist and the restless writer in me will probably impel me to abandon neutrality and seek in India as in England the true story and the proper ending.

3

November, 1942

[South America] It's 8.30 a.m. now, but you're having a hot lunch and how I wish I were there, with the rocking chair and the settle. Is Bombo living with you now like a good little husband? Or has he still got the call of the wild in his whiskers? But here is a wide lagoon with a hard ochre-coloured beach and peaked mountains running south to the end of the eye, with coloured houses and onion-towered churches lining the steep green cliffs with their red soil, polished date palms, the smell of paraffin that exudes from the calm oily water and lies heavy on the stairs and in the cabins and even in the artificial ventilating draughts, the native boys in their brilliant little surf boats painted banana yellow or crimson or sea blue; and all the motley of our march through the streets two afternoons ago while the ship was taking water before we slid out into the bay to wait for movement orders.

Oh, we had a huge parade through the streets. The locals were a little frightened at first. Then they realised we were British troops and they flocked like flies along the roads. We marched past the Governor in the main square, a beautiful garden of bamboos and lime and acacia and palms, and the black women mingled with the yellow and the white, cheering and making gestures of various meanings. In the doors of hovels naked babies with huge bellies and navels like eyes crowded and flapped their hands. Old shrivelled women made V-signs from their chairs, and all the girls with their pointed heads and thick lips, black frizzy hair and white teeth and eyes, clad in cheap glittering yellow or red American cotton frocks, danced and waved and dived into our marching threes to shake somebody's hand or give someone a fresh green orange or a new banana.

It was a strange riotous day. We came back in the dusk, with the thick green trees glowing lucently in the warm street lamps, with the doors of the cathedral open and all the profusion of baroque statues and golden altar clothes and burnished rails lit up by clusters of candelabra that fell also on the white frocks of the kneeling women. And all the flickering street advertisements like Piccadilly Circus, and the marines drunk and merry and the girls standing on the corner of the street of brothels. It's marvellous to see such a mixture of race and colour as in this melting-pot; they looked very healthy, though not as Amazonian as one might have expected.

In the evening they had a reception and my pet colonel A— met the dignitaries and discussed the world. The governor's wife made a speech in English, which she scarcely knew, praying that we all return unscathed soon, soon... and she burst into tears. So we evidently pleased our new planet.

4

November, 1942

I'm tired today, very tired. I've been rushing around a good bit and never getting many hours sleep. I sleep on deck, which is forbidden, I wait till midnight and nip up in my shorts and lie on deck in my waterproof bag from Ravens, and look up at the heavy rounded shape of the lifeboat and the stars and the moon and suddenly I find an old wizened sailor with a sweeping brush in his hand shaking me gently and saying '6 in the morning sir, decks to be washed'. And there is the sun, in all its early glory, and the sailors cascading hoses of water down the deck. And I lean on the rails and the wind goes through me with delight. But I think I need more sleep and less of these 'ere discussion groups and Hyde Park Corners. I lectured to the intellectuals with success this week and this afternoon I took some colonial officers to the men's side of the ship for our Hyde Park weekly and we had a rollicking two hours' parliament on the Dominions and the chances they offer the white man. And little George, the boy who wanted to divorce his wife in Southend because she was whoring, and who joined the army at sixteen after trying to go to the colonies, he gave the loveliest talk I've ever heard, in his singsong illiterate unaspirated Welsh voice, about the Jewish collective farms of Palestine which he'd seen when he was shooting Arabs out there. 'No one grows for money, they breeds beautiful 'orses and they got lovely orange groves an' the doctor don't ask for money for 'is services but you pays 'im with food or clothing or whatever you do make. An' I never seen a 'appier people in my life an' by God I wished I could 'a stayed with them.' I felt the loveliest feelings while he spoke as if a little child were telling me some quaint and innocent story rich in human goodness and all the richer because it was so artless and unconscious.

5

December, 1942

[Durban] It was an experience of some moment to spend two afternoons and evenings ashore in South Africa. A large city of skyscraper flats and pseudo-American stores, degraded knick-knack shops, plenty of cinemas and hotels, and integral with this conscious Western mode a bastard kind of native life. Rickshaws pulled by Kaffir boys in loincloths or denim trousers, all barefooted, trains reserved for Europeans, cinemas and concerts likewise: black boys aping the white in blazers and pipes and the swear words they've picked up from the Tommies; a native bazaar with all the stench and colour you can imagine, great olive brown women with nothing on but a rope skirt and a tall brown beaded tribal hat, babies tied to their backs, little wizened natives sitting on the floor of booths full of dry skins and bones and seaweed, Indian women sitting with their delicate profiles and soft blue and pink saris selling potatoes on the pavements – it was very exciting. I went ashore with Gush and we enjoyed our stroll. Then a middle-aged couple, a bank cashier and his wife whose faces I've already forgotten, asked us to have a cool drink in their flat and we went for a drive in their Austin 7 the next afternoon to see the countryside. The white people are all very concerned about their future vis-à-vis the black tribes who are educating themselves so fast and growing unruly against the restrictions that society imposes upon them, and also vis-à-vis the Indian community who came originally as coolie labour but are now exceeding prosperous and universally hated and debarred from society, from buses, cinemas, dances everything. So they build their own cinemas and buy their own cars and settle in village communities where they grow vegetables and bananas and mealies for sale in the city. It's an amazing instance of peaceful penetration, of a new element working

13

harder and living cheaper than the original inhabitants and becoming its economic rivals. I don't agree with those of my friends who say they'd like to settle in South Africa after the war. I think it's got much savager problems to settle than Europe has and I doubt whether they're heading towards a solution. You can't educate and suppress a people at the same time – if you do, you repeat the battle of India.

6

December, 1942

I want to write a poem tonight. Do you remember the poem that echoed and echoed after we read it?

> The bailey beareth the bell away;
> The lily, the rose, the rose I lay.

I was on deck after dinner, night had just entered upon the sea and the sky, and I had just shaved off my moustache in a sudden fit of mirth to think of my black moustache under an enormous topee. Anyway there I leant against the rail and the night wasn't deep enough for the water to become phosphorescent, but the crescent moon was riding along on our port bow and inside the crescent was the veiled remainder of her circle, and the sea was a vast estate of restless moonlight. And two lines formed in me – these two lines:

The moon in her gentleness
Meekly companions us...

And no more have I found, seeking patiently for what must follow. I can't reach it, Gweno, any more than I can reach you. Do you see how a poem is made – or fails? By perpetually trying, by closer and closer failing, by seeking and not finding, *and still seeking*, by a robustness in the core of sadness. What else is there by which we can live, now, you and I? We won't surrender, by God we won't. Don't we know how wonderful the world is, and how foolish, how incredibly foolish mankind is? But we can't give up what we have. That would be so very foolish that no one would even take pity on us. Let it beat its fury – we'll stand against it. Yet I feel exhausted by the day to day slowness and normality of the ways of men – such men as we are here on this ship. I feel tired to death of myself, of my not knowing, and of my wanting to know. I did an hour's reading after breakfast – the geography of Asia. Before breakfast I stood on deck in my pyjamas after sleeping on the boards under the Southern Cross and the Pleiades all night and the cool utter freshness of sun and breeze soothed and refreshed me. I watched the occasional flying fish sway lightly and swiftly over the chopped blue sea. Then I shaved and had bacon and scrambled egg. Then I went and swam, did some P.T., and after that I tried to get the water out of my ears (I'd been trick-diving) – and dressed, and went along to give the second lecture of a series on the war in the Far East. The boys sat on the burning deck just like in the poem, and I stood in a bit of shadow on the bridge and expatiated, with the help of my blackboard and the lovely map in coloured chalk, on the industries and histories and ideas and climate and ambitions and qualities of Japan, China and Burma and Malaya and the romantic diseased islands of the Archipelago. And though the sun beat on them like a glass eye, the boys seemed to be lapping up my garbled wisdom as if it was pink lemonade.

7

December, 1942

Once again the day of the sacrament. It's only seven weeks, yet it seems like a lifetime, really it does, since I said 'Goodbye darling', at the door of the dark bedroom. Oh time is long. And yet this voyage has been so placid in a way, it's been a complete seclusion of the spirit despite its crowded cabins and decks and messrooms; there's been only the sea, and the sun, and the moon, the ship's steady voyaging and the ultimate purposes all far away, never touching us, distant as the distant horizon. That is why I've been able to write so much poetry; and why, now that I've given up my Entertainments job and sought a few days' freedom before the shrieking chaos of unloading our mighty luggage from half a dozen holds and directing the coolies to load it on to the train, I am living in a world of pure contemplation, letting daily life revolve on the circumference of the circle, while at the centre my thoughts and emotions form their altering patterns and make their music. I'm drawn in to the tones and phrases of this long mood – so that the two lines

> The moon in her gentleness
> Softly companions us...

keep me fretting and striving for two whole days to reach the rest of the poem that I knew at once *belonged* to those lines and would be born if I could let it find its difficult way out of its narrow tomb.

INDIA

8

Boxing Day, 1942

We had a 'Dog and Stick' march this morning – no work –
just rolled off in groups with a series of rendezvous, across
the hills, over the dry sandy river beds, by the deep stone

19

wells through the tumbledown villages, up another steep granite scarp that was so like home, down past a tiny little shrine set in the desolate plain with a small stone Buddha protected by a heap of stones. I stood by Buddha for a long time, trying to understand. But it was no good. I only knew that it was closed to me as long as I was a fussy little officer sahib with a hundred unimportant jobs on his mind: and no peace to discover slowly the intricate paths to the universal tranquillity that gives unbounded freedom. 'Whose service is perfect freedom.' I hadn't realised what a magnificent phrase that is, yet I've repeated it hundreds of times in church.

But to continue, we trudged across the flinty parched plain, past the shepherd and the sheep, to a little lambing pen like the one we saw in Nacton that spring evening behind Queenie's and there again was a little shrine, very modest and quiet. And carved on red stone were two horsemen on a horse with a dog. Perhaps a traveller's shrine. The little pen had about twenty newborn lambs and six gambolling furry little puppies. We tickled them till they stopped howling and then we went on through the village to the canal where those of us who could swim had a lovely cool bathe in the swift muddy water, diving from the stone bridge into about twelve feet of water and swimming against the current as hard as we could go. That was the coolest hour since the rain stopped on the first night. What a welcome we had that day, after travelling all night, and unloading our baggage, seventy tons of it, from one gauge railway to another in pitch darkness. We had to work in an incessant downpour till long after dark loading our lorries with luggage and sending them splashing over the mountains to our camp. Finally the road became hopelessly flooded and one of the trucks got bogged in a swirling torrent that rose in half an hour and roared across the road. We were an hour trying to shackle it up to another truck to get it out. We succeeded at last and blue with cold and dripping like gutters after hours of drenching, we plodded our way home through waterlogged trucks to find in my case neither clothes nor food. So I stripped and towelled myself and got into the bed old Tudor had made for me and slept like a babe. I'm no whit the worse for the adventure either. Isn't it amazing?

And now I'm sharing a tent with Tony Lewis and we've planted a sort of yellow broom in front of it and we'd love to invite you to tea.

9

New Year's Eve

I'm very despondent tonight: which in the great field of Morale (beloved word to the military mind) is a serious, nay, a court martial offence. I'm sitting like Brutus in his tent (I'm not as worldly wise as Cassius) with a hurricane lamp besieged by crickets and tiny fleas that bounce in from the long mud stretch that goes away from my wall-less tent into the hills. All the tent flaps are up – I've just got a canvas roof on poles and across the flats the Indian soldiers are singing their native songs and soon the jackals will come howling and prowling seeking the dead sheep and bullocks that lie rotting among the black and grey beds of silt. And it's the last night of the year. I can't let myself imagine what you're doing. The bugle blows lights out in the darkness. 10 p.m. – five o'clock in Aberystwyth. You've had tea and are sitting round the last cup from the brown teapot. Bless you all.

...Why was I so despondent? Oh, because I'm sizing up the realities of the situation. I've been censoring letters all the week: it's a daily duty now, to censor all the scout troop letters. They're all dutifully cheerful. 'Well, here we are, mam, in our new home. Settling down very nice, don't worry.' Or what is worse, to go reading and reading, love letter after love letter, sentiments that sound so depressingly banal when other people utter them in the tritest English you can imagine. And something in me is kicking against the pricks. I want more freedom than I possess. I want to get away by myself. I get tired so quickly of the conventional life of the Mess, the officer-mind and its artificial assumptions, the rigid distinctions of rank which so rarely go with quality or character, the backbiting and watching each other that is a seething obligato to our daily bread. It's an arid society, and when I realise that it governs this vast continent, I don't wonder at the results which are only too apparent in every village I pass through. A sudden soft breeze stirs my lamp and soothes my hot face. I wonder whether it means rain. The night is moonless and dark despite its array of stars.

What is Life? What is Life? Now I'm writing like a little man in Chekov. The remedy is always the same. Discover what is exciting or laughable in the immediate. Alright.

We went for a route march yesterday and saw a flock of grey monkeys leaping among green trees about a village temple. On the way back we bathed in the swift yellow waters of the canal. One of our boys swallowed a lot and began drowning. I dived in with another man and got him out. Forgot about it till now. In the evening I sat on a Ford V-8 engine and watched the fitters strip it, to learn a bit about it. Then a dull night in the Mess and a long gossip in my tent till midnight. Today (P.T. as usual in the first cool hour. Then map-reading and Bren gun instructing. One corporal very sick and in pain with colic – got him an ambulance and packed him off with his pay book and shaving kit to hospital) we went over the hill to our neighbouring regiment and inspected their scout cars, after which we drove them round the hills and plains just to get the feel of them. A very young, burly, fair hair, blue-eyed English officer met us – he's having a thrilling time. He's only been out two years. Some of the other officers are in their tenth year. One of them is a celebrated gentleman jockey – very charming and distinguished looking – the ornament of a fin de siècle.

Went back to camp and was told by the Major that, alas, I am Messing Officer for the squadron with effect from today. Native cooks, bad fish, burial pits for waste – a job any man would run a league from. It's mine! A change from lecturing the intellectuals of the Athlone Castle on Education in the New World.

Saw the Indian wallahs in the cookhouse – one man works for nothing but his meals, chopping wood. Another sits all day peeling potatoes for 6d a day. He does it very, very slowly and I said 'Karo tezi, tezi' ('Do it quickly'). The Indian sergeant with a big belly and eyes like paraffin was most impressed. 'You speak proper Indian, sir,' he said. 'You've been how many years in India?'!!

I missed my own tea (but bought four annas worth of tea from the charwallah who sits on the ground with an urn of tea kept hot by charcoal burning under it) and took my grey bathing shorts and went for a bathe to the canal with Tony Lewis. Arrived there, we found the canal was dry – the sluices had been opened and the fields irrigated. The green crops looked splendid but the canal was an awful sight – muddy banks and filthy boulders. However, Indian dirt always has its beautiful surprises and there was the most vivid kingfisher you've ever dreamed of, a wonderful, brilliant little flying rainbow, sedately watching us and the native boys who splashed themselves in the black water like sparrows in a puddle.

We walked on past the muddy village where naked children, black as soot, ran out and grabbed our hands and begged with white teeth for tips. Tony had an eight anna bit which is a working man's wage for two days – so one naked little grub beat his father hollow as a bread winner for once. The vultures and kites were sitting on a dead hill over the thatched and huddled hovels. They didn't move as we approached. And there was a rotting cow, horribly decayed. We hurried down the hill and native women carrying babies, or bundles on their heads, started running to get past us before we crossed their path. And so through the millet fields and the broom back to camp to throw a bucket of water over each other, standing up naked outside the tent. And on with trousers and shirt and up to the Mess tent to eat soup and bully beef and potatoes, and herring on toast. That's my day. No gossip, no interfering with anybody, no ambition, no nothing.

10

December 31, 1942

Perhaps, in the fullness of time, you'll describe how you spent the same few hours of our allotted span, Gweno fach. God bless you darling, and keep you well and may love keep you ever fresh and secret. And may I come back to you not too late, and the little ones come toddling out of Heaven to share our struggles.

11

January 26, 1943
In hospital, Poona.

My mouth is progressing quite well. I had it reset slightly on Sunday. I'll be very glad when I get out of here, and can open my mouth and speak and yawn and laugh again!

12

February 1, 1943
In hospital, Poona.

I wonder whether you'd enjoy this leisured existence of deck chairs and books, Gwen, and the sun as hot as a sword, and the white people all crawling into the shade? It's very restful if one's mind is at rest. I've had one or two spells of rest in it, but mostly I've been chasing my thoughts helter skelter through the universe. I think the resultant poems are probably more morbid than usual. I was reading my (your) Rilke this morning – he says a poet cannot write of joy until he has lamented; and that he has no right to lament unless he has the power of joy. I know I've the power of joy in me: you know it, too: so Rilke *will* authorise my black tone poems.

I've bought a pair of suede boots with crepe soles for living in the tank; and had my fortune told and was duly

26

promised a long life and a happy one. I can't resist any native sponger who comes round, like the mongoose and snake wallah last week. It breaks the tedium.

13

6th S.W.B., India Command, April 7, 1943

I'm very fit and very happy as far as most things go. I cannot and never will get rid of the ache at Gweno's and your absence, and I shall resent every moment I am away. But work is work and war is war, and I have no complaints about my work or my regiment. The job I'm doing now was just made for me; it's interesting, exciting and independent. It's never the same from one day to the next, and I have the most exciting duties sometimes. For instance, I've just returned from a three-day 'voyage into the unknown', with a three-ton truck, a blanket, a box of tinned sausages, milk, butter, peas and beans, prospecting like an old boy of the Roaring Forties. Looking for roads instead of gold this time. I've taken that truck into places that made it sweat – up the winding stony bullock tracks that dribble across the mountains, up dry river valleys into the hills, along the shores of the great dam lakes that conserve Bombay's water supply – it's a lovely life. I'm picking up the local dialect slowly and can chat to the villagers quite nicely. I'd never find my way without them. Last night we were in a particularly remote wild part and I had to hire a native guide to take me over the hills to a village on the other side where I'd arranged to meet my Intelligence Sergeant. The villages are cleaner up in the hills and the people less spoilt. They have a temple as big as a church, no matter how small they are, the women always run away when they see us, the boys and men come warily round us and look at the car with a respectful curiosity. The headman of the village will come forward with a glass of goat's milk to placate us and negotiate the sale of eggs at a 1d. each (I ate them raw today because we hadn't time to light a fire). Sometimes we see a black naked man slipping through the bush with a bow and arrow – they are 'jungle-wallahs' and live by spearing fish or killing peacocks, etc. And this in an area with roads, buses, and power-dams; it's amazing. There are bananas and oranges ripening in the grove and lovely rich red flowers like roses with a smell like acacia. And in the most inaccessible places you'll find a string of bullock carts plodding slowly along some ravine with all the drivers fast asleep. We toot on the horn in vain sometimes and have to get out and shake the man to wake him! It's very exciting, true; but I can't ever grow used to the idea that this is ours. I feel utterly strange here, and I sense a perpetual undercurrent of hostility among the people. Some villages are very friendly, others cold and reserved: I don't know why. But I'm glad of the experience. The world is much larger than England, isn't it? I'll never be just English or just Welsh again!

...Gweno gives me copious news of my book's fortune and the various odd poems of mine that are floating around. I'm more interested in the ones I haven't written, and I'm itching to write now. I've sent her two short stories on airgraph sheets during the last month, and I'm still sitting on the long story I wrote in hospital ['Ward 'O' 3 (b)']. I don't know whether to send it or not. It's too 'all of one breath' somehow. And Gweno says the critics detect unevenness in my writing already. So I'd better leave it till the war ends, God knows how long it will be, though.

I hope Mair is well and getting on top of Manchester. It was lovely to read her account of spring in M/c – I remember so vividly the itchy dirty feeling spring gave me, and I used to sweat at the effort of the dandelions to burst through the flagstones! Bless the gal, I say. There's plenty of open air in these parts, anyhow!

14

April 17, 1943
Lake Karakvasla

...So I'm in my tennis shorts, sprawled on my bed, writing the first airmail letter to you since almost Christmas – it's not been worth sending letters before, because they took so long. But your last letter came in about six weeks, so I'll try this one with six poems that are more use in England than out here. I don't know what to think of them; I have a feeling that there's more simple poetry in them than any I've written – they aren't as pointed and severe as the hospital ones and they're simpler in their melody and wording. All of which is to the good. It's interesting (to me) the way they've evolved. I've had a few pages of jottings for the last fortnight but couldn't get anything out of them at all. Then, last weekend, I sort of had a mood. My head seemed to develop a spasm of music and lovely phrases appeared in the water. It didn't recur, but each night this week from ten to midnight I've sat down in my quiet tent and disciplined my thoughts successfully enough to hammer out these six poems from the raw material. There've been several versions of some. Each version I worked to simplify and abbreviate. I've cut out nearly every 'rich' adjective and high metaphor (damn this wind and dust) and in a casual sort of way reduced them to their minima. One of them ('Water Music') came just as it is, without even being asked. It was literally a 'gift'. 'Home Thoughts from Abroad' began at an open air camp concert last week when the cheap blue stage curtains billowing in the wind, the trumpeter playing St Louis Blues, in the light of lorry head-lamps, which were the only footlights we had, and the dark starry sky above us engendered a sudden brief excitement in me that I've tried to make the poem recover. Unsuccessfully, I fear.

'Bequest' – well, if you don't like it, Gweno, throw it away. I told you I was sending you something not happy at all. And although I'm more and more engrossed with the single poetic theme of Life and Death, for there doesn't seem to be any question more directly relevant than this one of what survives of all the beloved, I find myself quite unable to express at once the passion of Love, the coldness of Death (Death is cold) and the fire that beats against resignation, acceptance. Acceptance seems so spiritless, protest so vain. In between the two I live, I think you live, too, and I think the certainty grows gradually upon us – the certainty that we have exalted ourselves to an indestructible love. I feel it more and more, and it stops me being abject, but your old husband is so terribly anxious to get back to you that he hits out violently at any suggestion the poet might make to the contrary...

And yet, looking at the whole thing as a soldier purely and simply, I can't see the war out here finishing for at least three years. I've read everything I can lay my hands on about the Japs, to the tiniest detail. I've been to every lecture, and there have been some brilliant ones – and my sober conclusion is that they're as hard to beat as the Germans, every bit of it. There'll be no sudden end like a fairy story, and I try to husband my patience accordingly. But oh, it's a sad sad thought. So I think I'll go and have a swim for twenty minutes...

I can see a lot of white dots across the lake – they must be men: there's a hush hush camp there which plays a bigger part in Pacific history than most things. One of their fellows came over in the launch on Thursday to give us a talk on the Japs. As he'd been living behind their lines for the last seven months and has all the breezy flair for the bloody and exciting that Hemingway and the laconic American school have, he was very well worth listening to. He was an American himself and had seen so much death that he could afford to treat life as rather amusing. He kept us rippling with laughter at the same time as he lifted our hair into the air. Some guy. No isolation of the intellectual or conscious left-wingness about him...

15

April 27, 1943

And here's another early morning kiss to waken you in the depths of your Welsh night. Eight o'clock here – two thirty a.m. in your dreams. I'm beginning to despair of myself at night, for I've failed twice now to find a moment to write to you before bed. Yesterday and the night before, I was enticed, seduced and destroyed by the long octopus arms and hungry hard mouth of a shapeless poem that will never be written. It seized me with soft little thrills as I entered the tent, and each night till long after midnight, I've wrestled vainly with it in the long battle of thoughts and words. When I did at last go to bed I felt spiritually bewildered and unnerved, as though the thoughts had battered and exhausted me. And I knew last night, that I couldn't *live* with the thoughts that encircled this particular poem and I was afraid of being alone with them after I had put the lamp out. I lay in my sheet and tossed and groaned and fretted until, suddenly, there was Tudor shaking me and saying: 'They're going on P.T., sir.' So off I raced to do handstands and dorsals in the red dust of the first sunlight. I don't understand what happens in these matters. But I do know that one can be utterly alone with certain thoughts, and it can be very hard to endure, even if it's only for five minutes.

So I failed to write to you tonight, and now the morning is as busy as ever and I write a sentence and then dash off to see the C.O., and return and write another, and then cycle off to get Platoon positions from the Companies going out on a 2-day exercise. Then a third sentence and in comes an officer with a truck and an unexpected request that I accompany him to survey a stretch of ground where we're going to do our field firing... 'I've only got an hour to do it in, and I can't do it unless you come. I don't know any other officer with sufficient mastery over himself to say Yes or No to a problem and stick to it.' I was, in a quiet way, very thrilled because I've never swapped confidences with Freddy, we've just knocked about at work, that's all. I don't believe it myself because I'm too willing to see the other side of the question always, and the possible alternatives. But I'm glad I don't *appear* vacillating.

...I'm longing to hear from you; surely I'll hear today. But whether your letters come or not, I do not for a moment lack the warmth and truth of your love. It's a wonderful thing, and it sustains me always and always. I don't often sing about it, though I whistle Jesu Joy in the mornings, and murder Cherry Ripe and Snow White too. I've got two black robins in my tent each morning. They perch on my books and look in the mirror and ruffle their wings and peck their images. And drop their little ordure on Spender and Shakespeare and the Bible and sing like angels, but like *angels*.

16

May 9, 1943

It's nice and shady here, under the awning, in a basket chair, empty tea cups and sandwich plate on the table, in the same place as I was last Sunday tea time, Bombay Cricket Club. It's a large cricket ground with huge concrete stands all round like a football ground – and this is a sort of enclosure with tea rooms and club rooms. The Indians own it and allow the whites to patronise it. The whites sit and drink tea stolidly. The Indians all play cards and talk. The whites are all men, the Indians have their women with them. The mixture of dress is odd – some in European clothes, some in saris. They're a funny lot, as if they were sitting on the hedge, conscious of both the East and the West. They look a bit nervous, we a bit bored. They've got a sort of dubious over-confidence, we the stolid uneasiness of soldiers of occupation. Really I loathe and detest the whole gambit. I *could* be happy in India, but only if Britain and India were good friends. If we were out here as, say, Auntie Connie and Uncle Ernie have been, and India was really growing into a maturity such as we have at home, then I'd enjoy all that *is* enjoyable here. Now I run through the list of pleasures and am doing nothing more than killing time. For instance today, being our day off from training, I stayed in bed instead of going to breakfast, and then took a long stroll in my Bukta shorts, along the dusty track leading inland from the beach. The country is very, very ugly in detail there. That is, looking at it all it's a very fine spectacle of inland creeks, palm-forested hills, swampy fertile fields and villages on each dry eminence. But when you walk and look at it, it's mud and the slithery chameleons and crabs of the mud, decaying houses and bad smells, dirty garbage humps with black crows cawing on them. And the sun beating the dust finer and finer. I strolled with my sweaty hands in my pockets for three or four miles as far as the little Catholic mission school in the village where the natives wear English frocks and handbags and parasols and worship God and speak bookish English. Then I turned back to the beach and felt a bit dizzy with the power of the sun. There's a little ferry service by the beach where the big single-sailed local craft tack across the creek and the old rickety bus jolts up, the customs officer examines the passengers, the gramophone croons tinnily at the soft drinks counter, and the children ask for tips. I sat and sat there, watching the human antics, and then returned to our own part of the beach to join all our officers in the water. Then someone said 'Coming into Bombay for the afternoon?' And before I had time to say No, I said OK. So... We've been rushing round Bombay doing things all afternoon. We took a taxi after lunch and went to Crawford market to try to buy some pugree silk for you. The shops were all shut, so I looked at a few razors, and then we went into a big mosque, leaving our shoes on the steps. It was very simple and clean and cool, I liked it. No carving, no pulpit, no stained glass. Just large window spaces and little kneeling mats on the floor for the believers to kneel to the East. And a pool like a swimming bath full of goldfish where they wash before praying. I'm indifferent to religion these days because I feel hard with myself, and because every desire I have is a selfish one – the desire to survive, to exist, to find you again. And I don't think God is interested. So I didn't look at the mosque with any true eye, but just as a stranger looking at the customs of others.

I don't know how the rest of the evening is going to pass. I suppose we'll eat and go to the cinema. It doesn't matter much. If I'd stayed in camp I'd have read some poetry and tried to elucidate some of the hard passages I've jotted down during the week. I spent all Saturday night trying to find the proper words for one single simple four-lined verse, and failed. I don't mind the effort, in fact I enjoy it, but I think it's as well to throw myself away from it, like a ball on a string. That's why I'm in Bombay. (That and the simple restlessness that is a permanent state of mind now.)

17

May 14, 1943

How I've contrived to write any poems I don't know, nor have I any idea where they come from. I wrote a long prose poem two days ago at midnight quite without toil or heart-searching. And then I couldn't sleep all night.

18

May 26, 1943

...Thank you for the love in your letters, and for the gossip too. It's so comforting to read about the lilac and the kindling sticks and Denny's mushrooms... And my heart seems to be at home in my body... Oh Gweno I'm tired for the touch of your hands. I'm so tired *of lacking that springing joy*. Gweno, death doesn't fascinate me half as powerfully as life: you half hinted so when you mentioned that Koestler article on Hillary, but you know really, darling, how I turn insatiably to more and more life, don't you? Death is a great mystery, who can ignore him? But I don't *seek* him, oh no – only I would like to 'place' him. I think he is another instance of the contrary twist we always meet sooner or later in our fascinations – like the atrophy at Llangranog when we walked up the hill in the dark and that you with your Life spirit battled so hugely to dispel, astounding yourself I know. And again at Aber, on the hillside that Easter before we went to Borth y Gest. When again you were big enough to take me as a stranger and 'make' me again – and isn't Death a stranger that one 'takes'? So much is strange in all things – the essential virtue in such strangeness is courage – to test, and endure and abide by what so slowly and surely emerges. I talk only as one who has been fortunate – the song of a man who has won through, as D.H. Lawrence said. And has found his mate. And what else need worry the essential *me*, darling? All the rest will happen and is happening. Well, if it must, let it. I still sing and can hear you singing, too, your Songs of Sleep and Snow White and the Swans, and that's all I want of all this. Give me that and I can achieve all I have the potential to achieve.

19

May 28, 1943

It's 10.30 on Saturday night. I would be about calling in Control to collect you, instead of sitting here in pyjamas in the usual humid warmth, having censored a pile of airgraphs and been quietened and humbled to see how simple and innocent men can be, especially the ones who write clumsily and misspell and omit verbs. The one saddening thing in all these men's letters is their nostalgic references to good times they used to have and followed by what seems a completely illogical rider to say that doubtless 'they'll come again'. It's like the same thin dance tune played over and over on a gramophone, and it makes me feel that we are as powerless to direct the future as is the writer of 'Bluebirds over the white cliffs of Dover'. The other universal trait is the tendency to strike a semi-heroic attitude over the training we do – superhuman endurance, blood curdling heat etc. – and I suspect myself of shooting the same line. It must read very silly to all the dear anxious people who read these marvellous epistles. I suppose I must be tired, to be seeing things as if they're washed in Lysol. I am a bit tired tonight, too. It's Saturday and we're working today and Sunday on training. The soft sand and the mud on which we do our stuff takes it out of you a bit and I just lay on my bed from 6pm to dusk and dozed in a warm retrospective dream in which it seemed I had only to put out my hand to touch your arm by your elbow, but I wouldn't do it because a touch would have set fire to too many emotions – and I couldn't bear it. *I just couldn't bear it at all.* It was the outer circle of a poem, if you like, but I made no real attempt to pierce to the kernel and take up the intolerable struggle for the honeycomb of words. So in the end I went for a stroll under the ragged rainy sky down to the edge of the traeth and the waves were just like Penbryn's curlers with the same ruffle of wind on them. I don't know, Gweno, I don't know anything. I just feel tired of the present run of things. I went up to supper – corned beef and tomatoes – and had a gin and lime to dismiss my introspection...

The mess is much pleasanter now than it ever was in England, principally because we are thrown entirely on our own company, and I find I have got a lot of genuine friendship there, even when dear Gush is away on a course. I don't lack friends in the battalion, and the men are real comrades to me, especially my own Intelligence Section who are a nice mixed bag – a Kent schoolteacher; a rough little Cockney boy with the intelligence of the East End; a Swansea University student with a happy go lucky freedom and a natural interest in life, who bites his nails and is untidy and never combs his short curly hair and is utterly reliable on duty and can march or endure with the best; an Irishman from Dublin as big as an oaktree with a dry dignity all of his own; and my inimitable Lancashire Sergeant, J. Hardman Green, who has a rough and ready turn of wit I can always rely on. I could give a hundred other vignettes of my odd brethren from South Wales and all over, and I find more and more and more that we are all living through an identical experience in the same way – all of us cherishing the same simplicities, afraid to lose the same things, and willing to share the same tasks and the same anxieties. Will we get the same reward? No. Some of us will get jobs, others disability pensions, others unemployment relief, others road labour, others nothing at all except darkness. That's the way of the world.

20

June 3, 1943

...I had a typed a/g from Howell Davies repeating his willingness to read the new poems. He, like some of the Swinnertons and other critics I've read, display a fussy interest in me and my fortunes – will my sympathies broaden, my understanding deepen, am I plunged too soon into this mammoth jungular world of the East, will it rid me of my own-ness, my close absorption in my own love and being? Etc, etc.. I react to these proddings by searching myself and concluding that everything is in the lap of the gods and I will feel and do whatever I happen to feel and do – but I shall make no conscious effort to broaden, extend, alienate or resolve myself. All I try to do, now I'm in midstream, is to keep afloat and keep going for the shore. What else can I do? Perhaps I can break the intensely personal chain of anxieties and longings that binds me so often, but I wouldn't for my life break any of the personal loves that are the basic strata of my little molehill. Ought I to?

The battalion still fails to satisfy my affections, engrossing and exacting though it is. It's changing a lot these days – a new C.O. and a new adjutant now, several promotions but none for me who am a long way down the seniority list: lots of men sent to other units because the training is too severe for them; new men joining from commando and paratroop units disbanded in the M.E. and Burma. One of them, a paratroop, swam across the river last night in pitch dark when the tide was at its fiercest. It was a river crossing scheme by night. I was responsible for the actual crossing and was paying out the rope as he swam. I was up to my neck in the rushing water and the last rope on my hand when he whistled from the other side – O.K.! I was *so* relieved – the river was so dark and swift and he'd been gone so long and I couldn't hold on any longer. He was a sturdy lad, old 20 Evans. Sometimes this training business ceases to be just sort of school work and becomes the real thing, and it sends a shiver of reality down your spine because it may go right and it may go wrong and you don't know till it's over. A sort of crisis in your body and mind as you watch events rapidly developing – and yet you stay as cool and matter of fact as if you were buying groceries.

21

June 18th, 1943

Thank you for your lovely pile of lettercards and a/g waiting my return from my long and exciting journey. I am glad you are having such a good life – London, Russian aesthetes, Llandrindod, oratorios – keep it up, I'm convinced there's nothing like putting your daffodils in water! It's no good taking life seriously these days, or it would be just too much. And don't waste your emotions in anxiety. We three boys are in a very big movement, and the security of centuries of British government is being put to the test in our case and everybody else's. And I think they'll manage to look after us and give us every chance. What can't be helped must be allowed to happen. I don't feel like a rat in a trap, nor does Huw, who sent me a charming letter this week – nor does Glyn, altho' he is more at war with the fates than any of us. I think the Lewis family are sturdy enough for most things...

I loved my journey – it was such a liberation to have nothing but the road, day after day, new sights and glimpses, hasty meals of corned beef and tinned sausage cooked at dusk and dawn on the verandah of the little bungalows the government has built for travellers to use along the endless roads. We saw tribes of gypsies with little mousey grey donkeys and a couple of enormous camels to carry their few belongings, and great palaces of the Indian princes, palaces as splendid as Hampton Court, and medieval fortresses in the little feudal native states where, to my astonishment, I bumped into a herd of chained prisoners watched over by Ghurka sentries. And rivers in flood that somehow we managed to drive our little jeeps through, and jungle tribesmen slipping through the trees with bows and arrows, thin brown soft eyed men like antelope, and beautiful peasant girls beating their saris clean at wayside pools and running away if we stopped to examine the road or the bridge. It was a colossal experience and I feel I could go on travelling like that for years, yes literally for years. My mind stayed in its proper place, my imagination was content to watch the Marco Polo wonders of ordinary life, and my body was just part of the car and the speed. No wonder I feel disconsolate on returning to earth.

I had Elizabeth Bowen's review yesterday and The Listener's too. I am very cheered by them and couldn't ask for better. I don't think I'll stop writing as long as I live – I feel as if there's a steady fountain with a good head of water in me, and without trying to be pretentious, I think I can do my duty to thought and word and life...

Thinking back on my own writing, it all seemed to mature of a sudden – between the winter of 1939 and the following autumn. Can't make it out. Was it Gweno and the Army? What a combination!!! Beauty and the Beast!!

22

June, 1943

I've been working hard at the short stories: mainly some new ones I'm trying to write. My touch isn't at all sure: my thoughts wander instead of crystallizing and I can't imagine the people objectively enough. So I've had to scrap several versions. I've written one three times, another twice, and I'm still dissatisfied. It's good practice, even though it's rather disheartening when I've got so little time for writing at all.

23

July 8, 1943

Thank you dear for so mothering my poems and trying them so assiduously. I didn't think *The Times* would touch the itching warmness of England's hand – no siree – nor Village Funeral, either. They want Virgil's imperial gaze these days, but not for me, because I don't see the splendour at close quarters, I see something much more bitingly real and distressing and inescapable. And that's all I'm concerned with saying, just the way it is and will be. And now I know I won't be able to wake up in the morning when Tudor pulls my net up and shakes me, for it's *late*, little princess, and there is only sleep in the world, and love in its hard shell, like a tall fruit.

Darling Gweno, goodnight my sweetest wife.

24

August 9, 1943
Lahore

[re his new volume of poems] I think it's better than 'Raiders' Dawn'... but it must be *different* as well as better. 'Raiders' Dawn' was young and passionate. These poems must be steadier, more general, more in line with fact and universal experience. Till they become that, I'm willing to wait.

25

August 9, 1943

...Lahore is sultry and parched. When I woke up this morning, in my compartment, the occupants of last night had gone and there was a beautiful old village priest with a brown soutane and a white beard, old and fragile, with silver spectacles – a Catholic Belgian priest. We talked very happily together in French, and very simply each of us stated the fundamentals of our roles, the priest his, the soldier his. He said gently, 'You lack our consolations, my son'. It was lovely to see him when I woke.

26

Karachi
August 12, 1943

I'm very lonely up here – I don't know why this particular batch of new faces and things should make me sad and disconsolate, it's happened often enough in the last three years. I suppose it's just the turn of the wheel. But I didn't want any strangenesses; I wanted to be with my own Welsh boys, though they have no roofs or hot baths or cinemas or bearers to polish and fetch. All the creature comforts are here and I loathe them all. I feel now that the only place worth going to is the Jungle. I've been here two days now and am recovering from the long journey. It's nearly all book work here, and I find it very relaxing to be physically idle for a change. I enjoyed doing nothing on leave, because it was such a liberation to laze and forget all about the tough world. I have such a lot to do here that I become ice-cold and get into it like a robot. It's been like 'seshies' this week – reams of map enlargements and précis, strategic plans, an essay and a map on Burma, and a language test in French. I shake it off like water, but it stops me writing. The course is intended for staff officers, but I've told them already that I want to return to my own unit. They raised their eyes to find someone who didn't want promotion! I could do with the pay of a staff job, which is vastly more than I get now, but I'd rather be poor and honest.

But how I do talk! And all I want is to be quiet. But there you're not here; the stone wall again. Tell me about London; did you sit in St James's Park and watch the ducks and talk to little soldiers, or go to the picture galleries? I still feel angry with both of us for not buying that beautiful Toulouse-Lautrec last year – it would have been a joy for ever and ever and we left it there! Oh dear. I wish we were ensconced in Chris' little granary now, not flung out into the sprawling gamble of big empires grappling for blood and oil and palm nuts. Peace sometimes becomes very hard to find. But you must not have these awful fears, you give me the jitters or make me want to slap you. I tell you we can't afford to imagine – let the mind dwell and the end comes. I'm getting tough, so must you. Take it easy, take it hard. And if sometimes my letters stop coming for a month or two or three, you'll still take it easy. I guess I've got too much to write and fight for to be scraped off the dish by this particular rough house.

27

In a bomber
August 17, 1943

We sailed over the desert like a vulture, and in the barren waste far below me I saw a little tree-fringed oasis among dead hills. I looked it up on the map when I got back. A leper asylum! Bless it! All, all alone, like Shangri La.

It's hard to know where the truth lies, isn't it? When disaster comes people forget what the war was being fought for and only want the gunfire to finish and the living to be saved. I'm thinking it's a job for brains as well as bullets.

28

Karachi
September 1, 1943

I don't know whether you've received the poems yet. They're a queer batch, written in queer moods over a long period, transplanting myself from India to Longmoor and Burma and the Never Never Land, and living more lives than are, so that they are a sifting of imagined lives and other people's experiences as much as my own. I've written one long poem here, but it's far from its finished form and I don't know when I'll get the clarity I need. My brain is too busy here and is restless and nervy without any of the deep brooding silences that are necessary to this trade of poetry. I don't think I'll come back with any big bombs – more probably with no poetry at all. You'll have to search for it in my desert. I'll be pretty hard bitten by then, maybe. Oh, why this temptation to peer short-sightedly into the future? I don't know.

29

Karachi
September 5, 1943

Thank you for your darling letter I had on Sunday when
I returned from a gloriously lazy morning at the Boat Club.
I was delighted by your vituperations against the sexual
preoccupations of my typewriter – breasts, breasts, breasts
you roar in a splendid Presbyterian Wesleyan rage. Well,
unfortunately, the world is full of breasts. I can't help it any
more than you can. And where there are human beings
there's sex. And I just write how I see things – and I see a
lot more sex than I ever write. And as for the Welsh miner's
son – I'm sorry you're cross with him. (There's a delightful
squirrel running down the fire escape, quick and beady.)
He may be a bore, but he's authentic. I know him, and he's
a touchstone for the other characters I'm not so sure about.
And I make no apology for repeating myself any more than
I would blame D.H. Lawrence, or Spender, or Hemingway
for repeating themselves. It's unavoidable. So if you want
to sever connection with the firm of Lewis and Lewis, well,
so long! Do you curse me now for being a) callous b) a
legpuller c) pig-headed or d) unfair? I'm chuckling to
myself, sitting on a stone floor in the sun letting my body
get brown after a tedious and busy day in the classroom,
and I don't chuckle so often as to despise a bit of fun. But
seriously, I see no hope of my writing maturing or getting
more objective, and if it upsets you I apologise but cannot
help it.

We had a busy weekend – I loved sleeping out again; this time in the beak of a cliff with the Arabian sea pounding like a great white angel on the red sands below and Scorpio curling his starry tail over the southern sea. I was quite tranquil, sitting listening to the familiar homely sound of the sea, as if I was a boy dreaming of God knows what in Penbryn with no idea of what he could do or couldn't do in life. I couldn't feel desolate and outcast and lost with the sea to sing to me, not even if I were Robinson Crusoe. The sun was very strong during the day and I burnt my back, and I had a lot of work to do too. I came back feeling as if I'd had an exhausting Bank Holiday at Barry Island! But the desert is a weird and wonderful place, and the exquisite rocky bays out there are so fresh and innocent. In one there were two Arab fishermen mending their nets: nothing else there at all. I stripped and went into the great curling waves for a swim, and sang and snorted like a seal. I love the immediate contact with the wild sea – it sweeps away all the longing and worry and doubt that so assails us these days.

30

September 15, 1943

It seems to me that wherever I go the world over I meet people somewhere or other who are lovely and animated conceptions of some original and beautiful Idea. I like to feel that is so, anyway.

31

Karachi
September 21, 1943

I've got very interested in the war in the East, not only as a purely military problem, but also because these countries and peoples are a constant source of wonderment to me: so strange and individual and unlike our closed swift little Western world are they. Every time I look at an Indian peasant, I feel tranquil, especially when we are on some fantastically strenuous exercise, for the peasant is so utterly different and settled and calm and eternal that I know that my little passing excitement and worries don't exist in his world and are therefore not universal and will disappear. I don't think I feel the same tranquillity in the starving villages of Bengal where there are such dreadful sights of human destitution, but over here, now that the hills and villages are beautiful and festal with the lush rains, the people are also beautiful to watch.

It really is an amazing, spectacular land but something seems to have gone wrong at the root of it. I sense a perpetual undercurrent of mockery and hostility towards us among the people. I've been reading a good book by Edward Thompson on India, a deep, careful and disturbing book which caused me to think that there'll be no peace with the Indians until we've fought them – I feel very sad about it all, for my heart is in the right place and I don't agree with the Britisher School nor the Churchill School. I feel this problem is too vast for us. I wish I had come here as a doctor, teacher, social worker: anything but a soldier. It's not nice being a soldier in India.

32

6th Batt. S.W.B.
September 30

And here I am, I keep saying to myself. After so much travel and motion, here I am. I feel uncertain about here. It was a tremendous emotional tug, a crying loyalty to the Welsh soldiers when I was away. I refused that job which meant 900 rupees a month and a real mental and physical challenge, because I wanted to be back with these boys. And now I'm here, I feel that it was sentiment and selfishness. They are lovely. Tonight, after playing soccer, I was having a bath in the straw sheds of the showers. There was a resplendent yellow sunset with a great rainbow flung over the sky; and a boy was singing beautifully as the water splashed over him. I couldn't see him, but only hear his voice.

And yet I want to be away, too. It's time I took a harder job in a way. Yet I'm frightened of leaving them. They seem to have some secret knowledge that I want and will never find out until I go into action with them and war really happens to them. I dread missing such a thing; it seems desertion to something more than either me or them. When I was leaving Karachi, one of the instructors said to me, 'You're the most selfish man I've ever met, Lewis. You think the war exists for you to write books about it.' I didn't deny it, though it's all wrong. I hadn't the strength to explain what is instinctive and categorical in me, the need to experience. The writing is only proof of the sincerity of the experience, that's all.

And the country is so beautiful now, the rich crops and the long fields of yellow sunflowers and red currant flowers and the peasants look so fertile, too. The rains make the burning cruel earth into a green gentleness of fruit and leaf. Soon it will all dry up again. I dread the long merciless months ahead.

33

October 11, 1943

I know this won't reach you till mid-December, and that it won't leave my possession for nearly a fortnight, and that you'll be waiting in vain for the least mousy squeak from your vagabond Mickey. But it's only another proof that the world wasn't made for us, and we mustn't expect too much of it. It gave us a great deal once. Perhaps it'll start giving again some day. But just now it isn't giving anything away, and I can't even tell you where I'm squatting at this moment, nor what I'm looking at. I wasn't up by the mountain lake long enough to recover the feeling of communion and sympathy with the place that I felt so strongly when I was there last Easter and wrote the Water Music and Shadows sequence. The brief fortnight I did spend there was such a turmoil and rush of schemes that I never had time to be 'myself' at all. I bathed in the lake twice and felt its gentleness covering me then, but as soon as I returned to our lines it was gone, and I was aware only of jobs and irritations and constrictions. I do want to write: I'm sure there are several deep-water poems swimming about below the surface. And there's a whale of a story in the air, something big-boned and definitive, placing objectively the balance that swung in the monsoon of the Orange Grove. I don't know whether I'll be able to write it. There are too many gaps in my knowledge of India and too many failures in my sympathy, I'm afraid; but I've been re-reading Passage to India and I do feel that I should try and state the same themes in terms of the war against Japan and the effect of the Burma Campaigns on the Anglo-Indian community which I've had a chance of observing in the Nilgiris and in Karachi. It's an interesting theme psychologically; and it has enormous symbolic possibilities. That's why I'm not keen on attempting it. I welcomed the desire to write the Orange Grove, because it was so purely personal and rhapsodic; this larger theme has a greater responsibility of judgment in it, and requires more time. As if I ever get any time! Anyway, it's not my way to talk about things if I intend doing them. Usually I don't know anything about a poem or story until suddenly I discover that it's written itself, and I'm left with a slightly incredulous and pleasantly surprised tiredness. I feel more and more that my metier *is* writing: that that's the only real thing I can do. I can be a moderately good soldier, but not *very* good, because I have too many scruples and a certain detachment from it all that tends to undermine my physical energy and enthusiasm. Moreover, I find my memory in my 29th year, is taking a new and definite shape to itself. It's discarding everything it doesn't need to write and dream upon. It retains the bare necessities of soldiering: otherwise it forgets. All the stuff I learnt at College and Pengam has gone by the board, and it tunes itself more and more to the simple human material of life and of itself. It won't even acquire the economic statistics of the Beveridge report, the newspaper articles, or Oxford pamphlets. It's going native, quite definitely, and all its reasoning is done from a human standpoint. My longing is more and more for one thing only, integrity, and I discount the other qualities in people far too ruthlessly if they lack that fundamental sincerity and wholeness. So I only hope that I will be able to write, for I'm sure I won't be able to do anything else half as well.

34

November 21, 1943

I told you I found a very fine periodical out here called *Man in India*? A missionary called Verrier Elwin living among the aboriginal hill tribes of Bengal, and a civil servant called W.G. Archer, edit it. It has translations of beautiful folk poems and love songs and marriage chants. I wrote to Archer – Elwin seemed too august and intense a figure just to write to as an outsider – and he sent me a charming reply inviting me to go and stay with them if I ever got leave. You'll love Elwin's book – *Leaves from the Jungle*. It's a brilliant laconic diary of the most primitive life and his own wit and bravery and faith, never expressed except in dry little anecdotes of lepers and syphilitic village girls coming and sitting on his dung heap – I would like to meet him. It would be a profound experience – like seeing a bit of God and being unable to commit myself to his service.

And now it's bedtime, all on my own I go. Hockey finished, censoring finished, darkness waiting to fold me away. Tomorrow is always a little itch in my head as I turn in at night. I don't want it very much. I prefer it to become yesterday.

35

November 23, 1943

I've just had your a/g from Maenclochog about the little Cockney Welsh boys: they certainly put me to shame. If you'd only sent me to Efailwen for a year, Daddy, when I was seven or eight, eh? I'd be a nice Cymro now – but probably a Welsh nationalist writing in Welsh like Uncle Tim – and none the worse for that, maybe. I regret my lack of Welsh very deeply: I really will learn it when I come home again. I know more Urdu than Welsh: it's very sad – it's the price you pay for an M.A. in medieval history at an English University at 21. If I could live my life over again one of the things I'd do would be to learn Welsh: another to do an English degree at Oxford or London, a third to work underground for a year, a fourth to marry Gweno. Well, perhaps none of these mistakes are fatal, and I may still pull things together!

When I come back I shall always tackle my writing through Welsh life and ways of thought: it's my only way: but I must get to grips with the details of life as I haven't yet done: the law, the police, the insurance, the hospitals, the employment exchanges, the slums: I've always enclosed myself in an impalpable circle of seclusion, turning away to the Graig or Traeth Bach for the aloneness that is some-how essential for youth to breathe and grow at all. But I hope I can breathe in crowds and in business when I return, for all these fields of human life – the greater part of people's lives in fact – is scarcely known to me – I mean in sufficient force and familiarity to write of it. I don't know whether I'll write much out here: one book maybe in the end. But my most serious and continuous work must be from home!

36

December 6, 1943

I don't know whether the new lot of poems are good enough. But Graves and Howell – two chancey sort of critics – have approved them. Shall I risk it? I can't make up my mind? Perhaps I'll be able to judge them by the time they finally reach me. There's no hurry in one way. In another way there is. But I've got a persistent feeling that I'm still waiting for my big moment, my big word. It's still in seed and won't flower till it has a mind to. I can't hurry that up.

37

December 15, 1943

Well, Glyn has gone back to his camp like a good little boy, and I to mine. It was nice to see him, in a ghostly way. We were thinking, though not saying, all the time, 'Mother will be delighted that we met'. And I was thinking, 'He's enjoying the comfort of a hotel and the meals as much as a trip to London and a night at the ballet for Mair.' He slept like a log in his sheets on Saturday night while I lay awake listening to the traffic and the drunken officers singing and shouting in the next room but one. In the end I got up and walked into the drunken party in my pyjamas and told them to pack it in. They were like sodden mice. 'OK, old boy, sure thing, old boy.' They split up then, and I heard them saying to each other, 'Thanks awfully, old boy. Jolly good time, old boy. All the best, chaps.' Fancy people being like caricatures, hundreds of them – our middle-class leaders! Still, they're not as dumb as they sound, and I don't hold it against them. But a Poona hotel is a fearful sight – like Blake's robin redbreast in a cage. Must write a short story about it!!! But Glyn touched me deeply. There was real pathos in his narrow short cheap trousers and simple shirt issued by the grateful government: and his quietness amongst all the toffs. He told me how he sees things – the authentic and bitter view of the ranker who has no mercy for his superiors and revels cruelly in criticizing them – which is all he has the power to do. And it is an unbalanced framework, too, Glyn with ten rupees a week compared with my seventy to a hundred a week. I find it particularly unbearable in troopships and troop trains, where the difference in comfort is glaring and appalling; oh dear, it's a bad old world, it really is. And is it really getting better? In so many way I feel it's getting worse.

38

December 22, 1943

I feel very near to you when you write so closely of your day and your thoughts: you're very real. I keep on realising that. Your reflections are always very closely related to what you are describing: and although you refuse to leap into the metaphysical or pensive as far as I tend to do, you make a deep impression by keeping your thoughts in the same proportion as the deeds. Like the overpowering effect Rilke makes with his 'small' poems – 'Isn't he hard on her? Isn't she rather young?' or 'He for her sake grows commensurate'. I always realise this when I'm trying to write a poem or a story – if I get too far away from the thing, the thought becomes flabby and invalid, and it weighs on me with a dead weight and all the creative vitality dies in me. Often I just feel flat and dejected as I write: and persist in writing and try to throw the defeatism off: but it wins in the end. You never commit that crime. I rarely do it without finding myself out. It's the person who deludes himself who is the whited sepulchre that every great mind has pronounced the arch-miscreant of life. And it's the only invariable proof of the necessity for and the real significance of truth. I don't mean the truth that a court of law looks for. I mean the texture of a person's life. I'm more careful about this integrity than about anything else, whether personal danger or advantage suffers. And although war is so monstrously arbitrary and violent that personal values seems as futile and ineffectual as 'art for art's sake' I still

hold them, like the thousands of others, because there is nothing else to save one or make one worth saving.

I went on a three-hundred-mile journey last week to look at the jungle. It was a unique experience. You enter a separate world, remote, unperturbed, indifferent, serene, and it makes your own troubles and fears fall away and remain outside in the world of roads and spaces. The peasants are different in the jungle hamlets. Little mud huts and plantations of bananas, a smooth space for threshing grain, a little temple with sheaves hung in a cradle like harvest thanksgiving, sturdy girls and spare smiling suspicious men. All in a dumb show. Like the snakes we encountered, they won't attack unless you threaten them vitally. And they don't want you. We killed a wonderful Russell's viper, *so* beautiful, too cold in the early morning to writhe away quickly enough: and the dew glistened on its lovely diamonded skin. We also startled a ten foot snake from the long grass and G. had three shots at it as it flickered across the clearing. He got it: and it curled up slowly and raised its fine little head above its shattered body and stared at us inscrutably till the Colonel slashed it with his stick and it was dead.

39

January 5, 1944

A great delight visited me today: someone came down from the battalion and brought two letters from you and the studio photograph and the delightful snap. I was so absorbed and far away from the officers sitting around me under the trees that when one of them spoke to me his voice sounded harsh and bullying, calling me back, and I felt angry and sad, having to reply to this Here, this Now. Thank you for sending me so much. And now I turn back to that secret message you sent me whenever I can and whenever I am in need; and whatever may happen, that will survive. It will survive me and it will survive you. It's something that no one can ever know. It doesn't need saving or pampering as miserable volatile me does. Oh, I get so angry with myself. Who am I? A strange uncommunicative creature. Let me just Be – 'the only minds worth winning are the warm ones about us...'

I've been fiddling about till it's after midnight. All the others are abed. They are coughing with the damp cold air and I find my hair wet with dew. I wish I could write all night. I've written such poor second-rate stuff lately. I wish I were alive, that part of me. But the most satisfying thing I do these days is dig a trench or hack a bamboo down or find that my compass calculations through the jungle brought me exactly to the spot I planned. I've been in the bush all day. There's a river of long idle pools and huge white boulders a mile or so in the forest. I've bathed in it every day so far. But as we broke on to it this morning on a compass march, lo! sleeping on a spit of red sand was a great crocodile! He slid into the pool like a quiet thought, hardly stirring the water.

It's such a bewildering country, parts of it are as peaceful and quiet as Penbryn – yet it contains all the coldness and pride of nature, elephants and bison, tigers, reptiles and insects. I love it. I love the little jungle villages with their circular mud and grass hovels and their little festivals. Yesterday we barged into a little dance in one hamlet. A painted cow decked in necklaces and bells and rich cloth was being led round the doors, and a man with a queer singing drum chanted at each door. I'm taking a villager out with me tomorrow to show me the edible roots and fruits. And C.R. is taking another to follow the sambur and jungle foal and get something for the pot. It's a strange easy interlude in my life, this January in the wilds. But I want life to become serious and purposive again. I want to be getting on, the way I must go to get back to you.

It's very cold for India and very late for me, so I'm going to give you a chunk of my love like chocolate and thank you again for your letter and snaps. Don't overwork, and don't catch 'flu, and don't be lonely...

40

January 9, 1944

I shall be sorry to leave this absurdly unreal little Elysium, but the wheel turns and we turn with it. Tudor and I spent all day hacking bamboo in the copse and making beds for ourselves. It was huge fun, and I've got a pleasant cluster of blisters from the effort and countless scratches from the angry bamboo thorns. I built myself a shelter deep among the trees, and a house too, and the little sweeper boys who are enrolled in the Army and go with the regiment, showed us how to climb the tall coconut palms, cut down a leaf and plait it into matting for roof or wall or floor. You can imagine the boyish pleasure of it all – and the unreality of it also, for I suddenly find myself thinking, 'What is happening – behind this?' And the dark foreboding comes with me to the river when I slip away to swim by myself and lie in the sun. I'm going down for a bathe now – the last one, too. Tomorrow I'll become filthy with the dust of roads and the grease and strain of a big motorbike.

And the night has slipped away: but it was a good night, for we've been arguing about the world, which is a cheering thing to do, for the usual talk in the mess gathers and dies over trivialities or personal teasing.

And while we argued under the trees at our trestle table, I could hear the villagers at their orisons. It was repetition of last night and I wished to be away among them and of them, for in the hyper-civilised world you and I belong to I've never been able to accept or discover a religion as simple and natural as I need. Last night it seemed that in that rhythm and clangour and steady chant, here was a rhythm of many universes and real truths. We went along the lane, the full moon clear and subdued, and the temple, a bare doorless building with mud floor and a stone with a primitive relief of a deity, was in the village clearing. A wick burnt in a cup of oil before the God, and cast its light upwards up the sinewy long legs of two rows of young men, and along each wall. They moved very little, a step forward and a step back, each man beating his hand cymbals in a rhythm that began slowly and gropingly as if approaching the unhearing God, and then swiftened to a thrilling tempo as the presence was reached and the shout of praise uttered in the final spasm of admission. At the end they cut a coconut in half, putting half before the God and cutting the other half into pieces like communion. Each boy ate a piece, including the tiny bambino who had clapped his little black hands assiduously all through the ritual. He had a peaked cap on because of the cold night and squatted like a little rabbit on the floor. And one of them came out and politely offered Jack and me a piece each. We were conscious of a communion as we ate it – and the God they were worshipping was Ganpati, the elephant, the God of Good Fortune. I hope it's a good omen. But these villagers are complete and uninhibited. They neither cringe nor beg nor sneer, and they don't avoid us at all. I feel very heartened by their simple greeting – and glad to find, if only for a few days, a humanity that imperialism and snobbery haven't spoiled.

And I've got a feeling that another phase of my life is ending now, and the climacteric is near. I'm glad, and I feel something working blindly towards a position from which it can see and plan, and have faith and work enduringly, not among things that crumble as they are made and meaningless in history and in the heart. Let it come: it's the old cry for the saviour, let it come. We need it so much.

41

January 15, 1944

I told you in my last letter that I might be unable to write for a few days, and life was certainly very fluid. I came back to the unit on a motorbike and had a day of bliss roaring due north up India, coasting down the Western Ghats, blazed and bleary-eyed with the sun and dust. That also is a form of escape, a suspension of thought in an immediacy of feeling and control. I got a wonderful feeling of experiencing and understanding, the bizarre and endless frescoes of horizons, hillcrests, millet fields, villages, markets, and the long slow streams of bullock carts loaded with little peasant families in their best white pugrees and best red saris, slowly ambling back from the festival or the bazaar into the vast dried countryside. One village had a great crowd which held me up. It was singing round a cart drawn by white oxen with a red canopy. And perched on the bamboo make-shift 'throne' was a splendid old Indian dressed in fine clothes, with a little man keeping his head from lolling, and the crowd beating and wailing and buzzing – and I realised suddenly that the old nobleman was a corpse. Isn't it a weird land? Oh, if only I had the composure and self-detachment to write of all these things. But everything is fluid in me, an undigested mass of experience, without shape or plot or purpose. And it is as well to let it be so, for it's a true reflection of this Now we scramble through. I've been reading Graham Greene's *Brighton Rock* and I feel a sort of horror at the gusto with which so many modern writers portray the detailed disintegration and instability and bewilderment of modern humanity. I'd like to wait until I can get a stronger and more constructive purpose to guide my pen.

42

January 24, 1944

When I consider how my days are spent! They go and go
and go. Nothing to show for them either. When I grow up,
perhaps I shan't mind so much! I've been trying to catch up
on my mail this weekend: I've written to Mair and Unwin
and Robert Graves and Gweno; and arrangements with my
bank, in the event of my becoming a prisoner of war, to
transfer my account to Aberdare. And I still have a horde
of jobs to do. Boohoo! It's a sort of holiday today, so I'm
writing to you instead of doing a rapid route march or
something strenuous this afternoon. And in the evening
I've got a hockey match to play and then I'll either write a
letter to Huw or go to the camp cinema and see *Stagecoach*
or tackle the enormous and reluctant short story I've been
mentally grappling with for some weeks. I've done one
good job this week. I've revised my collected poems for the
press. Gweno sent them out by sea mail. I received them
on Sunday and returned them on Friday. It was rather a
rush job and I'm not sure whether I've done justice to
them. Robert Graves was my mentor and guide and I
followed his detailed criticism very carefully. I rejected his
advice in some cases, but only after a long silent argument
in which I believed I'd proved my belief in the poems he
wanted me to cut out. Altogether they make fifty-two
poems – seventeen written in England, six at sea, the
remaining thirty out here. I suppose that's pretty good for
twelve months. More than I thought I'd written, for the

creative side of me has been pretty circumscribed by the life and surroundings I exist in now. I'm not writing any foreword for them: they explain themselves. I'm calling the volume 'HA HA AMONG THE TRUMPETS' (Job 39) sarcastic-like! I think it's quite a bright title though, don't you? I hope you approve of the book when it appears in the autumn and the copy Gweno gives you will have my love on the title page in invisible ink.

43

January 26, 1944

I've not heard from you this week: you'd be packing and travelling back, I know. And now the bleak term will be wrapping its grey shawls about you. Be strong against it, little pilgrim. It's not our doing, but we must see to it that it doesn't best us. Everyone is under a strain now, and I know I don't always make my letters cheerful. We know though, Gweno, don't we? We know how we stand in it all. I've put a huge burden on you always, through my poems, which have spoken more openly of the danger and the jeopardies than either of us could or would with the living voice. I don't want them to mean foreboding to you or to me. They're universal statements, if they're anything. They feel the world, and they mean all that is involved in what is happening. You and I acquired the right to our own destiny when we were together: we made our peace in the face of the unknown, and it will stand in despite. So deep

down we have no need to worry. I know we do: naturally:
like hell: but I can't tell you the peace you planted in me
any more than I can tell you I'll come back in the end. But
we're a tough pair of creatures, you and I.

I've been wrestling with myself a lot lately, and tonight
a clear voice in me said, 'Don't try and write any more. Let
them fertilize for the next few months. Forget about them.'
I don't know whether I can. I've not got sufficient
detachment to put one vital side of me in cold storage. But
it isn't much use writing now, I know.

44

February 2, 1944

Life is hopeless as far as living one's own part of it goes.
I've given it up as a bad job – midnight now before I turn
to Alun and drop the wretched Intelligence Officer. Last
night I was out on a night scheme. Next week I may be out
all the week. I wanted Dick to come this weekend but I
wired him not to because I'm too busy to get away and
dawdle and be myself with him. And yet I've got nothing
to show for it – no exquisite collection of intelligence cards,
no organization, no results. I suppose a lot depends upon
the field one is working in: mine is a field of destruction
which organises only to destroy. And although the Army is
supposed to have everything it requires, I'm jiggered if I
can equip my boys with the odd things they need. They

give us bicycles and pumps and lamps, but no connexions and bulbs! And so on: so what? We learn code after code, cipher after cipher: inevitably a new replaces the old. I think I'd prefer the 1914 type of war. It was more methodical than this one – and it ended before this one has really begun – for me. I don't think Germany can endure another year of war. I'm sure the Japs can hold out for a long time. You've only got to look at a mangrove swamp and stretch of jungle to realise that. But I'm not bothered about it – come what may, luck and endurance outlive the foulest day. I'm not going to write any more till the foulest day is behind me. Then I'll tackle a more massive fruit than any in the Orange Grove...

I must turn in now for I didn't get a lot of sleep last night. Will you accept me as being fit and brown and busy and no complaints except that I can't meet anyone I love and can't make any plans at all. I'm learning how much to expect of life – and making what I can of it...

45

February 17, 1944

This is my love to you first and foremost, and from twenty singing birds in a cherry-ripe pie of kisses whipped in the white of an egg. How's school? And the weather? And Venus? And Bombo? And you? Be you through thick and thin. I'm trying so hard to be me. And I will be.

I want to write you a clear glad message, late in the night, at the end of something and the beginning of something else. I'm writing out of clarity of spirit and letting Life have a chance. Not out of frustration tonight.

It's five days since I wrote to you, five dreamy days, characterless, indolent in the way only railway journeys can be. And we, nomadic and restless, wandering from one station to another, pulled up in sidings to eat our porridge or soya sausage (how the troops hate them!) or bread and jam, and scramble back when the bugle blows, and then sweat and try to digest our gobble while the train grins to itself and stands motionless for as long as it feels like not going yet! I don't mind a change myself – I live on changes these days, so I'm tranquil, and I'll describe our new camp to you when I get there with the usual calm observation of a placid tourist – as you described Maulbronn in your letter – which reached me just before we left our old lake and mountains. Only no Kepler will have scratched his name on no choir stalls out this way! We have a distinct shortage of choir stalls and scientists in India. I have a feeling that India will wake up to find far more Western things pouring into its flat and featureless philosophical voids than have done so yet, and it will play havoc with the balance of their lives, too. For instance, we passed an American construction company building a road out in the wilds and we halted nearby. The little beggar urchins came up singing, 'Oh Johnnie, Oh Johnnie, how you can lerve'. It's like influenza, this tinpot civilization that is so easy to export by radio and gramophone and film. And it's so demoralising too: it devalues everything, from true music to true love, doesn't it? It makes everything cheap and easy and immediate. Some people go into pseudo-highbrow raptures over Artie Shaw's clarinet, etc. etc... But I don't see it myself. It's like classy metallic furniture and cocktail bars and sophistication...

46

[In all previous letters I have omitted all personal and intimate passages, but after much consideration I have decided to publish this, his last letter to us, as it stands, because I hope it may help other parents, similarly bereaved, whose sons felt as Alun did about their homes but who, either by nature or through force of circumstances, had to be less articulate. I feel Alun speaks for them all. – G.E.L.]

February 8, 1944

Dear Mother and Daddy,

This is my big effort for the next fortnight: I won't be able to write a comfortable letter for a while, as time is rationed and we don't stay around very much in our training. I'm waiting for the leisure to compose myself and my mind, and I'll begin again when I get peace. But while we're training so intensively and are out on so many schemes there isn't much chance of keeping really and nearly in touch with you. So don't worry if I don't manage to write you a lot. I expect the same will go for Danny too as he has thrown in his lot with us. It's his birthday today and I wanted to spend the evening with him, but it was no good. All I could do was send a telephone greeting to him this morning...

We had a very peaceful day and a half. I stayed in Dick's room in the Officers' Hostel at Poona, a drab place with no furniture or washbasins or anything except two army beds. Not that we minded. It was a heavenly relief to me to have his rich reassuring familiar presence: and the time just flew away. There was a big cricket match opposite the hostel: we didn't stir to and see it: we just sat on the verandah and watched the people coming in and out. Dick loves to read and analyse any poems or stories I may have written: I disappointed him I'm afraid by my present sterility. We found time for a visit to the cinema – on Sunday afternoon of all times! Cinemas are a refuge from the heat: but this time it was more than that. We saw a very fine film – *Now Voyager* – with Bette Davis looking heartbreakingly like Gweno and going through a harrowing nervous collapse through the domination of a jealous mother. It was exaggerated in some things in order to press the moral home: but it was terrifyingly true in its portrayal of neurotic conditions as I know only too well; and I felt my very soul partaking in the struggle. It's rarely that I identify myself so totally with a film. It's eerie when it happens: your own life seems to depend upon what happens in the film, somehow, and you just hang on to each word and intonation with dread and hope. Do go and see it if it comes your way...

Dick had a copy of Keidrych's *Wales*, which I haven't read yet. I'm glad *Welsh Review* is coming out – Gwyn Jones has written to me twice about it, but I've got nothing to send him and I won't be writing any more for several months! Still, why worry? I'm not a sausage machine and if I can't write then it's much better to let things go their own way and get on with this deadly serious business of soldiering to which I'm so deeply committed.

It's very peaceful this evening, the sun and the shadows in the angles of the hills, and the crows and the odd voices carrying from soldiers chatting. I don't know why I'm so preoccupied these days – I seem to live with hooded eyes. I ought to say Ha ha among the trumpets and dash off and swim, but somehow I don't contrive. And Mair in her grey city would be utterly transported if she could breathe this sun and air and brown her body in its generous evening warmth.

Bless you, for your New Year's Greetings, mother and daddy. I feel the protection of your wishes for our strength and safety, and I'll carry them with me wherever the months take me. And you too look after yourselves, won't you, and look after Mair and Gweno. I miss you all very much, more than I can say or feel, and it's because you've enriched us with so much love and happiness and

guidance all the years we were together. The world makes
a boy tough: he becomes less generous, more suspicious
and cautious, but the boy you made is still as he always
was deep inside the shell of the infantry officer. And no
matter what happens to the infantry officer, my love and
my essential self will never be diminished, so purely was
it made.

Excuse this, if it hurts you. I only say it because it should
be said sometime. I'm saying it to myself more than to you.

And now I'd better do some more work and get some
supper before we go out on a night exercise, poor dabs!

> So long now,
> All my love,
> Ever, ALUN.

47

February 20, 1944

Here I am, nowhere in particular, sitting in momentary
comfort and peace under a fan with electric light. I've been
reading quietly by myself. I'll have to wait a good time
before your letters catch up with me. Happily, I don't feel
cut off from you by the mere non-arrival of letters, and as
long as you're not ill I always have a feeling of assurance,
nearer than thought or fact, of you being with me by day

and night, no matter what tempests and chances may blow. I would like to think you have the same comfort. Does it help you if I say you've rid me of the black mood and the distress of mind I have been labouring under? I'm just steady and square now and give as good as I get.

Don't send any more books for the present. When I settle down again, I'll ask for some. But not just yet. Maybe I'll ask you to come here yourself then, dreamer...

BURMA

48

Arakan
February 23, 1944

A hasty pot boiler to keep your hands warm. How are you? The sun is bright and gay and everything sparkling and scrubbed, and if it were ten years ago or ahead I'd have a gay scrubbed heart as well. As it is I philosophise and contemplate and remain neutral amid a massive hurry-scurry of regimental mankind. If by some magic we were together I'd tell you quietly all that I cannot tell you in a letter. The only things they permit me to say are the fundamental unchanging things that don't help the Japs or interest the 5th columnists: things of no consequence to the fighting world, the world of telegrams and troop trains and supply columns. But they sing out in my heart like a branch of cherries and seven singing dwarfs, louder than all the trumpets, and it's the only true meaning in the sunshine and the scene.

It's a limping, blinkered correspondence this, and until your letters catch me, onesided for both of us. But when you get it it becomes two-sided, doesn't it? And if you get this one and then get no more for a few weeks, it will be two-sided and complete. It must be. We must breathe freely, and keep our own world alive with sunlight and growth and health. The darkness and threats are from another part of ourselves. And the long self torture I've been through is resolving itself now into a discipline of the emotions and hopes of you and me and Shan and the Remington baby, and I can feel my reason taking control and working carefully and methodically. I'm becoming my job in a very broad sense and (I may be flattering myself) I feel my grasp is broader and steadier than it's been for a long time. I hope it's true, because that's how I want to be: and the rest of me is invulnerable. I want you to know that. I won't be able to do much about your birthday this year, except send my love by pigeon and whistle Cherry Ripe, and I'll get my little gremlin to put a shine on the knob of the kettle and spit into the kettle for luck. And we'll chalk up all the birthday teas and Xmas dinners we've missed and have them all in Greek Street and Charlotte Street in one luxurious and abandoned week in London.

As I write now, Indian troops are shouting and squabbling about their dixies full of dhal and chappatis and curry, and the air is trailed and lined with the smell of their food. Hobnailed boots clattering back and fore, and men asking questions, and birds flying over the wide blue sky. Last night I felt the moving active quality in the star-grown sky and the dark night and the silent watchful land – and there seemed to be a marvellous depth and freedom as well as danger and secrecy in it all. When you see Orion you are looking with my eyes. And the Plough tilts down on us both.

I must run now. Sorry I have to go. And God be in our heads and in our eyes and in our understanding. Buy me a typewriter when someone has one to sell, and I'll buy you a beautiful beautiful emerald or maybe a sapphire or maybe something neither of us knows.

SHORT STORIES

NIGHT JOURNEY

An hour before the midnight train left Paddington all the seats were full, the blinds all drawn, the corridor full of kitbags and suitcases and the burning ends of cigarettes. Several Welsh soldiers were singing 'Cwm Rhondda' and 'Aberystwyth' and the more maudlin hymns of the Evan Roberts Revival. Every compartment was hooded and blue with smoke. Just before the train started a young captain with the badge of an infantry regiment on his black beret opened the door of one compartment, a third-class one, and was about to make his way through into the corridor when a private soldier sitting in the corner said, 'Here you are, sir, squeeze in here.' He said, 'Thanks a lot,' and sat down. He was perspiring and dead white, he had no luggage, not even a respirator. He looked done in.

The crowded compartment looked at him with the same reserved inquisitiveness as the inmates of a small boarding-house covertly examine a new resident at his first meal. There were two WAAFs. The bespectacled one simply wondered why he wasn't travelling first and thought he looked distressed. The one with lipstick, who had been interrupted in her tale of her boy friend Bob, a pilot who didn't give a damn and was wizard with a kite, patted her set waves self-consciously and looked at him with wide filmstar eyes. The tanks corps sergeant-major, a young-sandy-haired man with facile features and the cocksure glance of the too successful, raised his fair eyebrows knowingly, discerning some irregularity. 'Good evening, sir,' he said politely. 'Good evening, sergeant-major,' the officer replied. Finally the RAF corporal and his companion, a blonde civilian girl cuddled close under his shoulder, disturbed themselves sufficiently to crane forward a moment before reposing again. The officer wiped his face with a dirty handkerchief and then noticed that an aircraftman was standing up in the compartment.

'I'm very sorry,' the officer said. 'You were here before me. I've taken your seat.' He stood up, deferentially.

'That's all right, sir,' the corporal said, craning forward again, the hooded light full on his Brylcreemed curls. 'He's a prisoner. I'm escorting him to detention barracks, sir. He don't sit down.'

'Oh, surely, that's not fair,' the officer insisted, still offering his seat.

'He's standing up on my orders, sir,' the corporal retorted. The officer shrugged his shoulders.

The train slid a little, imperceptibly beginning its long journey, then jerked forward with a puff.

'My God,' said the WAAF with lipstick. 'It's actually moving. Well, as I was saying, when I asked Bob to take me up, he said, "If you were fat and ugly I wouldn't mind risking it. But you – no, I won't risk you," he said. Sweet of him, I thought.'

'Maybe he just wanted something for nothing,' the sergeant-major said with a naughty gallantry.

'You men,' countered the WAAF, very haughtily. 'Your thoughts never rise any higher than your manners. Well, Bob isn't that sort, thank you.' She wanted to assert her value; she wasn't going to let him knock her price down; she sulked and considered what was best. The other WAAF was reading a Penguin.

'Got a penknife, sir?' the private asked. 'I've lost my cork-screw.' He had a bottle of liqueur whisky between his knees: he was evidently a man of importance in the compartment. They all looked at him, for the first time really; he'd only been a private soldier before. Now he had a bottle of liqueur whisky. The sergeant-major was the first to produce a knife. 'Here you are,' he said with alacrity.

'Thanks, major,' the private replied. He was a tall groomed man, with smooth hair, a big chin blue with shaving, a clever surface smartness in his nodding glance. He scraped away at the cork, smiling to himself. The WAAF hadn't considered him before. She looked interestedly at him now. After all, she hadn't actually cut him before.

'Would you ladies like a little chocolate while I'm opening this?' he asked, passing a box of chocolates round. The WAAF fell on it with little girlish cries of delight.

'Now, gentlemen, a toast to us all,' he continued, lifting the bottle to the light. 'You, sir, first.'

They all demurred; he reassured them. Sure, he had two more such bottles in his respirator, and 500 Players. They were welcome. 'Go on, sir. Sorry there's no wine-glasses. Nice drink, isn't it? Got connections, see, sergeant-major. Go on, drink it up. My connections wouldn't give me poor stuff, don't you worry. Come on, lady, drink to that pilot boy of yours. Come on, corporal, sweeten your breath. What? Not allowed to drink on escort? What a sense of duty. Blimey. Well, what about the prisoner. Come on, prisoner. Sweet as your mother's milk it is. Take a good swig now. I won't be calling round in the morning, you know. Oh, come on, corp, let the poor sod have a drink. Being alive isn't much fun for him. Yeh, why not?'

'If the prisoner's going to have one I don't see why I should go without,' the corporal said, anxious as a man who has bought a shirt too big for him and hurries back to the shop, blustering and dubious, to revoke the deal.

'Sure, that's the spirit, that's swell,' the soldier pattered. 'Now that's how I like it. We're all social now.'

'Or do you mean socialist?' the officer asked.

'Oh no, sir, begging your pardon, we're not socialist. Here's the capital, sir, here' – he patted the golden bottle – 'and wherever you find capital you find the black market, and wherever you find the black market you find yours truly, sir. I'm not proud of being a capitalist, sir. It's just an inescapable fact, that's all, sir. Calls for another drink, I think, sir.'

Here's a case, the sergeant-major's grin seemed to say, I'd like to get him on a fatigue, by God I'd shake him. He took a second draught with a friendly and local condescension.

'What shall I drink to?' the WAAF said coquettishly.

'You don't need to drink to anything,' the soldier said. 'You just want to drink, that's all, lady. However, drink to the rebuilding of Stalingrad, if you want to.'

'Why in particular Stalingrad?' the officer asked. 'Why not London?'

'Sure, London if you like. I don't mind. Every city's a job of work to me, sir. I'm an internationalist. Paid by America, Dupont of America, via the Chase National Bank – heard of it, sir? – no income tax on my salary, two thousand a year I get, sir. Before the war I put half the machinery into the Red October factory in Stalingrad, and I'll go and put it back in there after this little shake is over. I built factories in Magnitogorsk, too. Hitler won't see them, sir.'

'Say, you're talking big,' said the sergeant-major.

'Not particularly big, major. I'm small fry. Only I get around, you know.'

'And you're only a private, eh?'

'That's right, sir. I'm not ambitious. I'm all right. I've got connections in the Army. Got a living-out pass, got a suite of rooms in the Swan in Dorchester and a taxi to take me to camp every morning. I'm sitting the same course for the fourth time. Usually they send you back to your unit if you fail it once, but they're letting me stay on because I'm keen to get through, you know, real keen. Very comfortable down there. Course I volunteered for the Army, you know. Only I'm not ambitious, not like you, sir, or you, major.'

'Are you married, soldier?' the WAAF asked clumsily.

'Married, lady? What, me? I've got only the best wife in the world, that's all. Look, here she is.' He fished a wallet out of his trousers and hunted among the white five-pound notes for a couple of photographs. 'There she is, lady. That was taken in Shepheard's Hotel, Cairo. Here we are, both of us again, in the garden of the Grand in Bucharest.'

'You look much nicer in tails than you do in battledress,' she said.

'My battle dress wasn't made in Saville Row, lady,' he laughed. 'How d'you like my wife?' (She was a beautiful voluptuous woman in a glittering evening gown.) 'She's a fine wife. Sends me 600 Players a week, and I love her like I'd just married her, though I got a son of seventeen. He's in the States, he is, apprenticed to Henry Ford. Good kid he is, too.'

The stuffy compartment, overheated with the breath and talk and whisky, swaying a little with the advance of sleepiness and the unreality of the big names he flung out like attracting stars leaving their proper orbit, rocking with the gathering motion of the train, played a cartoonist's trick on them all. How absurd and how amiable they seemed, these little people with long and short noses, with vanities and illusions and daydreams, with their fatigues and desires and routines, their religion and bewilderment and pettiness! There was a gradual relaxation in them all, a common impulse to stretch their limbs and loose their guard. The WAAF leaned up against the sergeant-major; he took her hand; her regulation underwear crinkled the tight blue skirt against her thighs. He took her at his own valuation, pilot or no pilot. OK, big boy. OK, baby. The bespectacled girl let her Penguin lapse. She looked at the officer, dreamily, disinterestedly, as though there was something there that distressed her and wouldn't let her alone. Only the prisoner stood like a great dull bull, holding on to the strap, dark and swaying. His great sullen head and shoulders were in shadow, over-powering. He was a miserable devil. The whisky didn't seem to improve him at all.

'I'm an internationalist,' the private soldier said. 'I don't agree with wars between one country and another. I don't believe it. I got nothing against Russia. I worked there. Nothing against Germany. They're a smart lot, I take my hat off to them. America's the best of the bunch for a living. England's the salt of the earth. I didn't make this war, and I'm not fighting it. Ever had your fortune told, lady? I'll tell it for you with this pack of cards. OK?'

'I believe you're a fifth columnist,' the WAAF said lazily, snug in the sergeant-major's arms. She shuffled uneasily, paused, sat up, looked at him with a frown, puzzling over him. Certainty dawned in her silly eyes. She pointed a hand at him, hard and splenetic. 'That's what you are, you're a fifth columnist. I know you are.' Her hard grasping voice had the high pitch of hysteria. 'You can't fool me,' she jeered. 'You dirty fifth columnist. And they'll get you.'

'Aw, shut up,' he said. 'I never had no education but I

don't make a fool of myself in public like you, lady. Ever been in the Ritz?'

'What do I want with the Ritz?' she shouted, screaming with laughter. In the unreality of the moment the dark prisoner moved towards the corridor. The door was open into the corridor.

She was laughing uncontrollably.

'The fifth column dine in the Ritz,' she shouted, waving her arms and body from the waist upwards like a snake.

'Look here, lady, I never been insulted like this before. Look here, I got Commander Anthony Kimmins' autograph here, see? He gave it to me when we was playing billiards after lunch in the Ritz.'

'He's a liar,' she shouted, terrible tears in her eyes. 'They're all liars. Bob took me to the Ritz for a weekend, and I'm going to have a baby now, I'm going to have a baby,' she was weeping now, 'and he got himself posted to another squadron, he did.'

'Your prisoner's gone, corporal,' the sergeant-major said with the coolness of a man in the thick of mechanised battle.

'Christ,' the corporal gasped, suddenly white, his enjoyment of the scene sucked out of him. He jerked himself to his feet, pulling out a revolver. 'I'll get the swine.'

The officer pulled him back by the neck of his jacket.

'Put it back, you fool,' he said quietly, and slipped past the corporal into the corridor.

The Welsh soldiers were singing their national anthem in harmony, softly and most tenderly, alto and tenor and bass

moving back and forth like searchlights over the range of sound. The prisoner was leaning by an open window, looking at the misty moonlit fields.

'Hallo, prisoner,' the officer said. 'They've just missed you.'

'I was born just over them fields, sir,' the prisoner said, heavily, slowly, peaceably. 'See that level crossing there? Used to go over that to school every day.'

'Never mind,' said the officer. 'We'd better go back now. Both of us.' Both men sighed, and turned away from the misty white fields, and returned.

THE RAID

MY platoon and I were on training that morning. We've been on training every morning for the last three years, for that matter. On this occasion it was Current Affairs, which always boils down to how long the war is going to last, and when the orderly told me the C.O. wanted me in his office I broke the lads off for a cup of tea from the charwallah and nipped over to the orderly room, tidying myself as I went. I didn't expect anything unusual until I took a cautionary peep through the straw window of his matting shed and saw a strange officer in there. So I did a real dapper salute and braced myself. Self-defence is always the first instinct, self-suspicion the second. But I hadn't been drunk since I came to India and I hadn't written anything except love in my letters. As for politics, as far as they're concerned I don't exist, I'm never in. The other chap was a major and had a red armband.

'Come in, Selden,' the colonel said. 'This is the D.A.P.M. Head of military police. Got a job for you. Got your map case?'

'No sir. It's in company office.'

'Hurry off and fetch it.'

When I came back they were hard at it, bending over the inch map. The C.O. looked up. His face got very red when he bent.

'Here's your objective, Selden. This village here, Chaudanullah. Eighteen miles away. Route: track south of Morje, river-bed up to Pimpardi, turn south a mile before Pimpardi and strike across the watershed on a fixed bearing. Work it out with a protractor on the map and set your compass before you march off. Strike the secondary road below this group of huts here, 247568, cross the road and work up the canal to the village. Throw a cordon round the village with two sections of your platoon. Take the third yourself and search the houses methodically. Government has a paid agent in the village who will meet you at this canal bridge here – got it? – at 06.00 hours. The agent reported that your man arrived there last night after dark and is lying up in one of the hovels.'

'What man, sir?' I asked.

'Christ, didn't I tell you? Why the devil didn't you stop me? This fellow, what's-his-name – it's all on that paper there – he's wanted. Remember the bomb in the cinema last Tuesday, killed three British other ranks? He's wanted for that. Read the description before you go. Any questions so far? Right. Well, you'll avoid all houses, make a detour round villages, keep off the road all the way. Understand?

News travels faster than infantry in India. He'll be away before you're within ten miles if you show yourself. Let's see. Twenty miles by night. Give you ten hours. Leave here at 19.30 hours. Arrive an hour before first light. Go in at dawn, keep your eyes skinned. M.T. will R.V. outside the village at dawn. Drive the prisoner straight to jail. D.A.P.M. will be there.'

'Very good, sir. Dress, sir?' I said.

'Dress? P.T. shoes, cloth caps, overalls, basic pouches, rifles, 50 rounds of .303 per man, and grenades. 69 grenades if he won't come out, 36 grenades if he makes a fight of it. Anything else?'

'No sir.'

'Good. Remember to avoid the villages. Stalk him good and proper. Keep up-wind of him. I'm picking you and your platoon because I think you're the best I've got. I want results, Selden.'

'I'll give you a good show, sir.'

'Bloody good shot with a point 22, Selden is,' the C.O. said to the D.A.P.M. by way of light conversation. 'Shot six mallard with me last Sunday.'

'Of course we want the man alive, sir, if it's at all possible,' the D.A.P.M. said, fiddling with his nervous pink moustache. 'He's not proved guilty yet, you see, sir, and with public opinion in India what it is.'

'Quite,' said the colonel. 'Quite. Make a note of that, Selden. Tell your men to shoot low.'

'Very good, sir.'

'Got the route marked on your talc?'

'Yes, sir.' I'd marked the route in chinograph pencil and

the Chaudanullah place in red as we do for enemy objectives. It was all thick.

'Rub it all off, then. Security. Read his description. Have you read it? What is it?'

'Dark eyes, sir. Scar on left knee. Prominent cheekbones. Left corner of mouth droops. Front incisor discoloured. Last seen wearing European suit, may be dressed in native dhoti, Mahratta style.'

'And his ring?' said the C.O. He's as keen as mustard the old man is.

'Oh yes, sir. Plain gold wedding ring.'

'Correct. Don't forget these details. Invaluable some-times. Off with you.'

I saluted and marched out.

'Damn good fellow, Selden,' I heard the C.O. say. 'Your man is in the bag.'

I felt pretty pleased with that. Comes of shooting those six mallard.

The platoon was reassembling after their tea and I felt pretty important, going back with all that dope. After all, it was the first bit of action we'd seen in two and a half years. It would be good for morale. I knew they'd moan like hell, having to do a twenty-mile route march by night, but I could sell them that all right. So I fell them in in threes and called them to attention for disciplinary reasons and told them they'd been picked for a special job and this was it...

They were very impressed by the time I'd finished.

'Any questions?' I said.

'Yes, sir,' said Chalky White. He was an L.P.T.B.

conductor and you won't find him forgetting a halfpenny. 'Do we take haversack rations and will we be in time for breakfast?' He thinks the same way as Napoleon.

'Yes,' I said. 'Anything else?'

'What's this fellow done, sir?' Bottomley asked, then. Bottomley always was a bit Bolshie, and he's had his knife into me for two and a half years because I was a bank clerk in Civvy Street and played golf on Sundays.

'Killed three troops, I think,' I said. 'Is that good enough?'

I felt I'd scored pretty heavy over his Red stuff this time.

'Right,' I said. 'Break off till 19.00 hours. Keep your mouths shut. White will draw rations at the cookhouse. No cigarettes or matches will be taken.'

I did that for disciplinary purposes. They didn't say a word. Pretty good.

We crossed the start line dead on 19.30 hours and everybody looked at us with some interest. I felt mighty 'hush-hush'. My security was first class. Hadn't told a soul, except Ken More and Ted Paynter.

'Bring 'em back alive,' a soldier jeered outside the cookhouse.

Somebody's let the cat out of the bag. Damn them all. Can't trust a soul in the ranks with the skin of a sausage.

Anyway, we got going bang away. I knew the first stretch past Morje and Pimpardi and we did about three miles an hour there. The night was breathless and stuffy; we put hankies round our foreheads to keep the sweat out of our eyes. And the perpetual buzzing of the crickets got on my nerves like a motor horn when the points jam and all the pedestrians laugh. I suppose I was a bit worked up. Every time a mosquito or midge touched me I let out a blow fit to knacker a bull. But I settled down after a while and began to enjoy the sense of freedom and deep still peace that informs the night out in the tropics. You've read all about tropical stars; well, it's quite true. They're marvellous; and we use some of them for direction-finding at night too. The Plough, for instance, and one called Cassiopeia that you bisect for the Pole Star.

Then there was the tricky bit over the mountain by compass. I just hoped for the best on that leg. Luckily the moon came up and put the lads in a good mood. I allowed them to talk in whispers for one hour and they had to keep silent for the next hour for disciplinary reasons. We halted for half an hour on the crest of the watershed and ate our bully beef sandwiches with relish, though bully tastes like a hot poultice out here. It was a damn fine view from that crest. A broad valley a thousand feet below with clusters of fires in the villages and round a hill temple on the other side. Either a festival or a funeral, obviously. I could hear the drums beating there, too; it was very clear and echoing, made my flesh creep. You feel so out of it in India somehow. You just slink around in the wilds and you feel very white and different. I don't know... You know, I'd have said that valley hated us that night, on those rocky crests. Queer.

I didn't know which group of huts was which, but I could see the canal glittering in the moonlight so I was near enough right, praise be. The jackals were howling too, and some creature came right up to us, it gave me a scare. I knew that bully had a pretty bad stench. Anyway we got on the move again, Chalky White saying next stop Hammersmiff Bridge, and we slithered down as quietly as we could, hanging on to each other's rifles on the steep bits. We made our way between the villages and the drums beat themselves into a frenzy that had something personal about it. Then we went up the canal for about four miles, keeping about a hundred yards off the path and pretty rough going it was. Then we came to what I felt must be our objective, a cluster of crumbled huts on the foothills, pretty poor show even for these parts, and the boys were blistered and beat so I scattered them under the bushes and told them to lie low. It was only 5.30 a.m. and the agent fellow wasn't due until six. I had a nap myself, matter of fact, though it's a shootable offence. I woke up with a start and it was five past six, and I peered round my tree and there wasn't a sound. No drums, no jackals, no pie dogs. It was singing in my ears, the silence, and I wished to God we'd got this job over. It could go wrong so easily. He might fight, or his pals might help him, or he might have got wind of us, or I might have come to the wrong place. I was like an old woman. I loaded my Colt and felt better. Then I went down the canal to look for the chowkey fellow. I took a pretty poor view of a traitor, but I took a poorer view of him not turning up. He wasn't there and I walked up the path and just when I was getting really scared he appeared out of nowhere and I damn near shot him on the spot.

'Officer sahib huzzoor,' he said. 'Mai Sarkar ko dost hai,' or something. And he said the name of the man I was after, which was the password.

'Achiba,' I said, meaning good show. 'Tairo a minute while I bolo my phaltan and then we'll jao jillo.' He got the idea.

I nipped back and roused the lads quietly from under the trees and we moved up like ghosts on that village. I never want to see that village again. It was so still and fragile in the reluctant grey light. Even the pie dogs were asleep, and the bullocks lying on their sides. Once I travelled overnight from Dieppe to Paris and the countryside looked just as ghostly that morning. But this time it was dangerous. I had a feeling somebody was going to die and there'd be a hell of a shemozzle. And at the same time the houses looked so poor and harmless, almost timid somehow. And the chowkey bloke was like a ghost. It was seeing him so scared that put me steady again. He was afraid of being seen with us as far as I could make out, and said he'd show us where this fellow was lying up and then he'd disappear please. I said never mind about the peace, let's get the war over first, and I told Bottomley to watch the bloke in case he had anything up his sleeve.

We got to the ring of trees outside the village without a sound, and the two section leaders led their men round each side of the village in a pincer movement. All the boys were white and dirty and their eyes were like stones. I remember suddenly feeling very proud of them just then.

I gave them ten minues to get into position and close the road at the rear of the village. And then a damned pie dog set up a yelp over on the right flank and another replied with a long shivering howl. I knew things would start going wrong if I didn't act quickly. We didn't want the village to find out until we'd gone if possible. For political

reasons. And for reasons of health, I thought. So I gave the Follow-me sign and closed in on the huddled houses. There were a couple of outlying houses with a little shrine, and then the village proper with a crooked street running down it. The chowkey seemed to know where to go. I pointed to the single buildings and he said, 'Nay, sahib,' and pointed to the street. So I posted a man to picket the shrine and led the rest through the bush behind our scruffy guide. He moved like a beaten dog, crouching and limping, bare-foot. There was a dead ox in the bush and a pair of kites sleeping and gorged beside it. It stank like a bad death. Turned me. We hurried on. The bushes were in flower, sort of wisteria, the blossoms closed and drooping. We crept along under a tumble-down wall and paused, kneeling, at the street corner. I posted two men there, one on each side with fixed bayonets, to fire down the street if he bolted. The other two sections would be covering it from the other end. Then I nudged the chowkey man and signalled to my grenade man and rifleman to cover me in. I slipped round the corner and went gingerly down the street. Suddenly I feel quite cool and excited at the same time. The chowkey went about fifteen yards down the street and then slunk against the wall on his knees, pointing inwards to the house he was kneeling against. It was made of branches woven with straw and reed, a beggared place. He looked up at me and my revolver and he was sweating with fear. He had the pox all over his face, too. I took a breath to steady myself, took the first pressure on my trigger, kicked the door lattice aside and jumped in. Stand in the light in the doorway and you're a dead man.

I crouched in the dark corner. It was very dark in there still. There was a pile of straw on the floor and straw heaped in the corner. And some huge thing moved ponderously. I nearly yelped. Then I saw what it was. It was a cow. Honestly. A sleepy fawn cow with a soft mild face like somebody's dream woman.

'She never frew no bomb,' Chalky said. He was my rifleman. Cool as ice. His voice must have broken the fellow's nerve. There was a huge rustle in the straw in the corner behind the cow and a man stood up, a man in a white dhoti, young, thin, sort of smiling. Discoloured teeth. Chalky lunged his bayonet. The chap still had plenty of nerve left. He just swayed a little.

'Please,' he said. 'Have you got a smoke upon you?'

'Watch him, White,' I said. I searched him.

'Please,' he said. 'I have nothing.' He was breathing quickly and smiling.

'Come on,' I said. 'Quietly.'

'You know you are taking me to my death?' he said. 'No doubt?'

'I'm taking you to Poona,' I said. 'You killed three of our men.'

The smile sort of congealed on his face. Like a trick. His head nodded like an old doll. 'Did I?' he said. 'Three men died? Did I?'

'Come on,' I said. 'It's daylight.'

'It's dreadful,' he said. He looked sick. I felt sorry for him, nodding his head and sick, sallow. Looked like a student, I should say.

'Keep your hands up,' Chalky said, prodding him in the back.

We went quietly down the street, no incident at all, and I signalled the two enveloping sections together and we got down the road out of sight. I was in a cold sweat and I wanted to laugh.

The trucks weren't there. God, I cursed them, waiting there. They might bitch the whole show. The villagers were going to the well quite close.

'What did you do it for, mate?' I heard Bottomley ask.

After a long silence the chap said very quietly. 'For my country.'

Chalky said, 'Everybody says that. Beats me.' Then we heard the trucks, and Chalky said, 'We ought to be there in time for breakfast, boys.'

THE EARTH IS
A SYLLABLE

'What I say is, if you're in trouble, take it easy,' the
ambulance driver said. 'Always have done. Once I got a girl
in trouble and I wasn't going to get grey hairs over that.
And now I've bust the gasket and she won't budge and

maybe the Jap is nearer than our own boys, but there you are, you're no better off if your nose bleeds, are you now?'

He'd often thought he'd die; it was a familiar idea; why shouldn't he, if there's a war on and you're young and you try to be in it, somewhere? It had taken him a long time to succeed. He'd got into the army easy enough, but the war seemed to elude him all the time. If he was in England it would be in France in hot summer weather and he'd be eating Wall's ice cream outside the barracks. If he was in India it would be in Egypt and he'd think of the Eighth Army glowing in the desert, attracting him like a moth to its fiery circle. He used to fancy himself flying there like a queen ant on her nuptial flight and shedding his wings when he alighted, and going to ground there. And now that he had caught up with it, here in Burma, well, it hadn't been much of a show. But he'd never liked the idea of Burma. He'd always known he'd die if he caught up with it in Burma.

'Can't you stop tossing and kicking those blankets?' the ambulance driver said. 'Wear yourself out quicker like that. Take it easy, I say. I've been in some bad spots off and on. Narvik for a kick-off, and Crete for a birthday, and a bloody narrow escape from going into Libya with Ritchie; thought I was lucky once, being sent out here instead. But I reckon it's all the same where I go. There's sure to be a war there.' He spoke very mournfully, a sort of thoughtful incantation. 'I've had more crump than crumpet this war. That's why I take it easy, mate. You got to last a long time, you know. A long time.'

The driver had given up trying to repair the damage to the cylinder head of his 15-cwt. Bedford; the tropical heat and the dust of the bumpy track that cavorted through the misleading jungle had dried up his water and blown the gasket. It was useless. They were on their way to the rendezvous where the wounded from the advanced dressing-stations were handed over to the main dressing-station ambulances. Tomorrow they'd have to find out where the new rendezvous was; it changed daily, same as everything else changed daily; the situation was very confused, the Japs were said to have worked right round their left flank somewhere up the Sittang, and to have landed above Rangoon. Tomorrow they'd have to find out where the new rendezvous was, if it still mattered.

He was lying on a stretcher in the back of the truck and it was a bit awkward because the truck tilted steeply, one side in the ditch so as to let the traffic pass up the track to the front, what front there was. The rear flaps were strapped up to give him some air and he could see the darkness of the jungle encircling them. It was dark and soft like a mass of congealed blood. If you put your hand in it, it would give like a sponge. If the Japs were there they'd be sleeping. They had to sleep. Or a snake or a tiger would get them, they weren't all that clever. Any case you could hear them if they were there, calling each other like owls, because they were lonely, maybe. And the jungle was utterly silent, dark and shimmering with darkness like ebony, and malevolent. And he was quite at peace. He'd been more nervous in India than he was here. It was lonely in India, no friendship there, nor any active hostility to brace you. Just loneliness and strangeness. It wasn't dangerous there: just nerves, that's all. You couldn't walk into a native village and have a good time there like you wanted to. QUIT INDIA they painted on the walls. Quit India, the silly fools. How can we? India is part of the world. It's the world we can't quit. No, it was just nerves in India. Riding back to camp after the pictures in a trotting tonga with bells tinkling on the skinny mare's neck, it was so dark it was like riding to your death. Just nerves. Here he was quite peaceful.

There was a sudden murmur in the jungle, a sigh, a growing perturbance. Dust. The wind puffed up with a hot dry sigh and the dust came riding in on them in a thick irritating column, into their eyes and mouths, making them swear, sweat and blink and extinguishing the petrol cooker on which the driver was brewing some char. His own lamp spat a high flame and cracked the glass and then subsided. He didn't move. He liked the dust storms by day, the whirling cylinder of tall red dust moving across the plain, the moving red towers that touched the blue sky. He didn't like it at night so much; now when he put his hand over his face his skin was dry and dusty like a statue in a dilapidated museum, like an embalming. The blanket was filthy, it set the skin of his fingers on edge, and he saw with sudden distaste that it was covered with hairs and dandruff under his cheek. It made him think of his wife, she'd written to say he'd left some hairs on his pillows the time he was on embarkation leave and she felt terribly cruel to shake them off, she said. But she was so beautiful and fresh always and the house always so clean and simple, with the sun or the snow always lighting it. She wouldn't like this dust.

'Well, we'll have to go without a cup of you an' me,' the driver said, grinning and sweating as he leaned over the tailboard to stow the cooker away. 'Tisn't the first thing I've done without by a long chalk. Christ, I've been without work before now. That's a real nasty thing; being without work. I don't suppose you've been without work, chum, being an officer?'

His mouth was bitter and dry and it hurt him when he smiled. It was the lump the shrapnel had taken out of his throat was hurting now when he smiled. Life had been pretty heartless off and on, but you usually got a laugh out of it. When he'd written three novels one after the other and failed to sell any of them, and gone round to an agency for a job and the old clerk asked him if he could type and he said, 'Two fingers only,' and the clerk said, 'No good,' and he went to sea then as a trimmer. He'd never thought of dying in those days, though, it didn't seem a physical fact at all. Just something you wrote and theorised about. Not like this.

'Speaking for myself,' said the driver, 'I've found it a bloody sight easier with a war on. You don't have to bother now. It's all buttoned up. Food and clothes and dentists, trucks to drive, loads to carry, allowances for the missus. It's all laid on for you now. You don't have to bother.'

Yes, he thought, it's been pretty easy. You sink your scruples in conscription, and then there's always something interesting if you take the trouble of finding it. Infantry schemes, sleeping under hedges, swimming a river in full kit, being hungry, talking to a stranger. And since his regiment had been mechanised the tanks had him by the hair – the iron maidens – he'd never tire of pulling on the tiller bar and stamping on the clutch and pulling like hell on the gear lever and the thrill as she surged softly forward, grunting peacefully and bellying over a slope so sweet and easy. And the big 75 mm. gun and the voices of your friends in your headsets coming over the air. And the queer consolation of the other things he'd tried and written off for failures and now recalled – the little meetings he'd tried to run, debates round a hurricane lamp on the FUTURE, talks he'd carefully put together on RECONSTRUCTION, gramophone records he'd borrowed and played for the lads, the choir he'd tried to make something good of; naturally it was no good for a few odd men to sit round and discuss how to prevent another war, naturally they couldn't 'succeed'. Still, it was all right to remember it.

No. The terrible struggles had been quieter and less obvious than voyages and armoured regiments. They were just something inside you – simply whether to say Yes or No to a thing – to chastity or pity or love or drink with another man's wife. Maybe if you could avoid saying Yes or No to Life, and yet be free, you'd be stronger, better? Would you? How did the dust columns form? What did the Upanishads say? The Earth is a syllable.

'I'm turning in, mate,' the driver said. 'There ain't nothing I can do till a truck comes along. Get you back, then, if a truck comes along. It's so bleeding quiet in these parts, that's what I don't like. Makes you think we missed the road back somewhere, or missed the war or summat. I never did like the quiet. Give me a pub that can sell its liquor, not keep it. Give me a call if your pains come back, chum, though there ain't nothing I can do. Jesus, I'm tired. Goodnight, cocky.'

He stumped up the road a few yards to where he'd slung his mosquito net among the bushes. He sighed aloud as he pulled each boot off.

Now he was left alone and whatever he had he was alone with it. It was all right, as long as he was alone. Whatever he had he could manage it now. His lamp still burned calmly and it might last an hour yet. He didn't want the dark to come any nearer. He could see exactly where it started, just this side of his feet. And then it went on and on. The dawn is the head of a horse. He lay quietly among the crickets and the darkness and the moths came suddenly tilting head on against his lamp and righted themselves on his face, and flew on again. It was very still, except for the pain. There was a translucent golden influence at the core of his being. He could see his wife. She'd wanted a child before he left England, but it hadn't turned out that way. And now in a way he was glad. There was only her left, besides himself. She would understand. He'd tried bloody hard; he'd roughed it and now he was cut up a lot and he could smell the poison where his left shoulder and arm had been. But there was still her little house. That was all. He didn't want to go to Burma; he knew it would be a bad place for him. But all striving is a blind guess, and he wasn't in Burma now, he was in the night, in the common ground of humanity, and he wasn't alone now.

He wanted to get up and enter the darkness and enter the silent village under the hill and enter it with his wife alone.

Not in a tank, for that was a schoolboy's thrill, nor in Burma, because it was a bad place for him. So he pushed himself up on his spare arm and sweated all over; Judas! it hurt. But he hated the dirt and hair on his blanket, and being hot in bed and he wanted to have this little walk.

So he went across the plain in the night and the darkness was hot and tepid and after a while he didn't know where the hell he was; but he knew he was all right; and he loved her so much that he knew he could throw the darkness over the hill.

The driver found him five yards away from the truck.

WARD 'O' 3 (B)

I

Ward 'O' 3 (b) was, and doubtless still is, a small room at the end of the Officers' Convalescent Ward which occupies one wing of the rectangle of one-storied sheds that enclose the 'lily-pond garden' of No. X British General Hospital, Southern Army, India. The other three wings contain the administrative offices, the Officers' Surgical Ward and the Officers' Medical Ward. An outer ring of buildings consists of the various ancillary institutions, the kitchens, the laboratory of tropical diseases, the mortuary, the operating theatres and the X-ray theatre. They are all connected by roofed passage-ways; the inner rectangle of wards has a roofed verandah opening on the garden whose flagstones have a claustral and enduring aura. The garden is kept in perpetual flower by six black, almost naked Mahratti gardeners who drench it with water during the dry season and prune and weed it incessantly during the rains. It has tall flowering jacarandas, beds of hollyhock and carnation and stock, rose trellises and sticks swarming with sweet peas; and in the arid months of burning heat the geraniums bud with fire in red earthenware pots. It is, by 1943 standards, a good place to be in.

At the time of which I am writing, autumn 1942, Ward 'O' 3 (b), which has four beds, was occupied by Captain A. G. Brownlow-Grace, Lieut.-Quartermaster Withers, Lieut. Giles Moncrieff and Lieut. Anthony Weston. The last-named was an R.A.C. man who had arrived in India from home four months previously and had been seriously injured by an anti-tank mine during training. The other three were infantry-men. Brownlow-Grace had lost an arm in Burma six months earlier, Moncrieff had multiple leg injuries there and infantile paralysis as well. 'Dad' Withers was the only man over twenty-five. He was forty-four, a regular soldier with twenty-five years in the ranks and three in commission; during this period he had the distinction of never having been in action. He had spent all but two years abroad; he had been home five times and had five children. He was suffering from chronic malaria, sciatica and rheumatism. They were all awaiting a medical board, at which it is decided whether a man should be regraded to a lower medical category, whether he is fit for active or other service, whether he be sent home, or on leave, or discharged the service with a pension. They were the special charge of Sister Normanby, a regular Q.A.I.M.N.S. nurse with a professional impersonality that controlled completely the undoubted flair and 'it' which

116

distinguished her during an evening off at the Turf Club dances. She was the operating theatre sister; the surgeons considered her a perfect assistant. On duty or off everybody was pleased about her and aware of her; even the old matron whose puritan and sexless maturity abhorred prettiness and romantics had actually asked Sister Normanby to go on leave with her, Sister deftly refusing.

II

The floor is red parquet, burnished as a windless lake, the coverlets of the four beds are plum red, the blankets cherry red. Moncrieff hates red, Brownlow-Grace has no emotions about colours, any more than about music or aesthetics; but he hates Moncrieff. This is not unnatural. Moncrieff is a University student, Oxford or some bloody place, as far as Brownlow-Grace knows. He whistles classical music, wears his hair long, which is impermissible in a civilian officer and tolerated only in a cavalry officer with at least five years' service in India behind him. Brownlow-Grace has done eight. Moncrieff says a thing is too wearing, dreadfully tedious, simply marvellous, wizard. He indulges in moods and casts himself on his bed in ecstasies of despair. He sleeps in a gauzy veil, parades the ward in the morning in chaplies and veil, swinging his wasted hips and boil-scarred shoulders from wash-place to bed; and he is vain. He has thirty photographs of himself, mounted enlargements, in S.D. and service cap, which he is sending off gradually to a network of young ladies in Greater London, Cape Town where he stayed on the way out, and the chain of hospitals he passed through on his return from Burma. His sickness has deformed him; that also Brownlow-Grace finds himself unable to stomach.

Moncrieff made several attempts to affiliate himself to Brownlow-Grace; came and looked over his shoulder at his album of photographs the second day they were together, asked him questions about hunting, fishing and shooting on the third day, talked to him about Burma on the third day and asked him if he'd been afraid to die. What a shocker, Brownlow-Grace thought. Now when he saw the man looking at his mounted self-portraits for the umpteenth time he closed his eyes and tried to sleep himself out of it. But his sleep was liverish and full of curses. He wanted to look at his watch but refused to open his eyes because the day was so long and it must be still short of nine. In his enormous tedium he prays Sister Normanby to come at eleven with a glass of iced nimbo pani for him. He doesn't know how he stands with her; he used to find women easy before Burma, he knew his slim and elegant figure could wear his numerous and expensive uniforms perfectly and he never had to exert himself in a dance or reception from the Savoy in the Strand through Shepheard's in Cairo to the Taj in Bombay or the Turf Club in Poona. But now he wasn't sure; he wasn't sure whether his face had sagged and aged, his hair thinned, his decapitated arm in bad taste. He had sent an airgraph to his parents and his fiancée in Shropshire telling them he'd had his arm off. Peggy sounded as if she were thrilled by it in her reply. Maybe she was being kind. He didn't care so much nowadays what she happened to be feeling. Sister

118

Normanby, however, could excite him obviously. He wanted to ask her to go to a dinner dance with him at the Club as soon as he felt strong enough. But he was feeling lonely; nobody came to see him; how could they, anyway? He was the only officer to come out alive. He felt ashamed of that sometimes. He hadn't thought about getting away until the butchery was over and the Japs were mopping up with the bayonet. He'd tried like the devil then, though; didn't realise he had so much cunning and desperation in him. And that little shocker asking him if he'd been afraid to die. He hadn't given death two thoughts.

There was Mostyn Turner. He used to think about Death a lot. Poor old Mostyn. Maybe it was just fancy, but looking at some of Mostyn's photographs in the album, when the pair of them were on shikari tiger-hunting in Belgaum or that fortnight they had together in Kashmir, you could see by his face that he would die. He always attracted the serious type of girl; and like as not he'd take it too far. On the troopship to Rangoon he'd wanted Mostyn to play poker after the bar closed; looked for him everywhere, couldn't find him below decks, nor in the men's mess deck where he sometimes spent an hour or two yarning; their cabin was empty. He found him on the boat deck eventually, hunched up by a lifeboat under the stars. Something stopped him calling him, or even approaching him; he'd turned away and waited by the rails at the companionway head till Mostyn had finished. Yes, finished crying. Incredible, really. He knew what was coming to him, God knows how; and it wasn't a dry hunch, it was something very moving, meant a lot to him somehow. And by God he'd gone looking for it,

Mostyn had. He had his own ideas about fighting. Didn't believe in right and left boundaries, fronts, flanks, rears. He had the guerrilla platoon under his command and they went off into the blue the night before the pukka battle with a roving commission to make a diversion in the Jap rear. That was all. He'd gone off at dusk as casually as if they were on training. No funny business about Death then. He knew it had come, so he wasn't worrying. Life must have been more interesting to Mostyn than it was to himself, being made that way, having those thoughts and things. What he'd seen of Death that day, it was just a bloody beastly filthy horrible business, so forget it.

His hands were long and thin and elegant as his body and his elongated narrow head with the Roman nose and the eyes whose colour nobody could have stated because nobody could stare back at him. His hands crumpled the sheet he was clutching. He was in a way a very fastidious man. He would have had exquisite taste if he hadn't lacked the faculty of taste.

'Messing up your new sheets again,' Sister Normanby said happily, coming into the room like a drop of Scotch. 'You ought to be playing the piano with those hands of yours, you know.'

He didn't remind her that he only had one left. He was pleased to think she didn't notice it.

'Hallo, Sister,' he said, bucking up at once. 'You're looking very young and fresh considering it was your night out last night.'

'I took it very quietly,' she said. 'Didn't dance much. Sat in the back of a car all the time.'

'For shame, my dear Celia,' Moncrieff butted in. 'Men are deceivers ever was said before the invention of the internal combustion engine and they're worse in every way since that happened.'

'What is my little monkey jabbering about now,' she replied, offended at his freedom with her Christian name.

'Have you heard of Gipsy Rose Lee?' Moncrieff replied inconsequentially. 'She has a song which says "I can't strip to Brahms! Can you?"'

'Course she can,' said Dad Withers, unobtrusive at the door, a wry old buck, 'so long as she's got a mosquito net, isn't it, Sister?'

'Why do you boys always make me feel I haven't got a skirt on when I come in here?' she said.

'Because you can't marry all of us,' said Dad.

'Deep, isn't he?' she said.

She had a bunch of newly cut antirrhinums and dahlias, the petals beaded with water, which she put into a bowl, arranging them quietly as she twitted the men. Moncrieff looked at her quizzically as though she had roused conjecture in the psycho-analytical department of his brain.

'Get on with your letter-writing, Moncrieff,' she said without having looked up. He flushed.

'There's such a thing as knowing too much,' Dad said to her paternally. 'I knew a girl in Singapore once, moved there from Shanghai wiv the regiment, she did. She liked us all, the same as nurses say they do. And when she found she liked one more than all the others put together, it come as a terrible shock to her and she had to start again. Took some doing, it did.'

'Dad, you're crazy,' she said, laughing hard. 'A man with all your complaints ought to be too busy counting them to tell all these stories.' And then, as she was about to go, she turned and dropped the momentous news she'd been holding out to them.

'You're all four having your medical board next Thursday,' she said. 'So you'd better make yourselves ill again if you want to go back home.'

'I don't want to go back "home",' Brownlow-Grace said, laying sardonic stress on the last word.

'I don't know,' Dad said. 'They tell me it's a good country to get into, this 'ere England. Why, I was only reading in the *Bombay Times* this morning there's a man Beaverage or something, made a report, they even give you money to bury yourself with there now. Suits me.'

'You won't die, Dad,' Brownlow-Grace said kindly. 'You'll simply fade away.'

'Well,' said Sister Normanby. 'There are your fresh flowers, must go and help to remove a clot from a man's brain now. Good bye.'

'Good-bye,' they all said, following her calves and swift heels as she went.

'I didn't know a dog had sweat glands in his paws before,' Brownlow-Grace said, looking at his copy of *The Field*.

The others didn't answer. They were thinking of their medical board. It was more interesting really than Sister Normanby.

III

Weston preferred to spend the earlier hours in a deck chair in the garden, by the upraised circular stone pool, among the ferns; here he would watch the lizards run like quicksilver and as quickly freeze into an immobility so lifeless as to be macabre, and the striped rats playing among the jacaranda branches; and he would look in vain for the mocking bird whose monotony gave a timeless quality to the place and the mood. He was slow in recovering his strength; his three operations and the sulphanilamide tablets he was taking had exhausted the blood in his veins; most of it was somebody else's blood, anyway, an insipid blood that for two days had dripped from a bottle suspended over his bed, while they waited for him to die. His jaw and shoulder-bone had been shattered, a great clod of flesh torn out of his neck and thigh, baring his windpipe and epiglottis and exposing his lung and femoral artery; and although he had recovered very rapidly, his living self seemed overshadowed by the death trauma through which he had passed. There had been an annihilation, a complete obscuring; into which light had gradually dawned. And this light grew unbearably white, the glare of the sun on a vast expanse of snow, and in its unbounded voids he had moved without identity, a pillar of salt in a white desert as pocked and cratered as the dead face of the moon. And then some mutation had taken place and he became aware of pain. A pain that was not pure like the primal purity, but polluted, infected, with racking thirsts and suffocations and writhings, and black eruptions disturbed the whiteness, and coloured dots sifted the intense sun glare, areas of intolerable activities appeared in those passive and limitless oceans. And gradually these manifestations became the simple suppurations of his destroyed inarticulate flesh, and the bandaging and swabbing and probing of his wounds and the grunts of his throat. From it he desired wildly to return to the timeless void where the act of being was no more than a fall of snow or the throw of a rainbow; and these regions became a nostalgia to his pain and soothed his hurt and parched spirit. The two succeeding operations had been conscious experiences, and he had been frightened of them. The preliminaries got on his nerves, the starving, the aperients, the trolley, the prick of morphia, and its false peace. The spotless theatre with its walls of glass and massive lamps of burnished chrome, the anaesthetist who stuttered like a worn gramophone record, Sister Normanby clattering the knives in trays of Lysol, the soft irresistible waves of wool that surged up darkly through the interstices of life like water through a boat; and the choking final surrender to the void his heart feared.

And now, two and a half months later, with his wounds mere puckers dribbling the last dregs of pus, his jaw no longer wired up and splinted, his arm no longer inflamed with the jab of the needle, he sat in the garden with his hands idle in a pool of sunlight, fretting and fretting at himself. He was costive, his stockings had holes in the heel that got wider every day and he hadn't the initiative to ask Sister for a needle and wool; his pen had no ink, his razor blade was blunt, he had shaved badly, he hadn't replied to the airmail letter that lay crumpled in his hand. He had carried that letter about with him for four days, everywhere he went, ever since he'd received it.

'You look thrillingly pale and Byronic this morning, Weston,' Moncrieff said, sitting in the deck chair opposite him with his writing-pad and a sheaf of received letters tied in silk tape. 'D'you mind me sharing your gloom?'

Weston snorted.

'You can do what you bloody well like,' he said, with suppressed irritation.

'Oh dear, have I gone and hurt you again? I'm always hurting people I like,' Moncrieff said. 'But I can't help it. Honestly I can't. You believe me, Weston, don't you?'

Disturbed by the sudden nakedness of his voice Weston looked up at the waspish intense face, the dark eyebrows and malignant eyes.

'Of course I believe you, monkey,' he said. 'If you say so.'

'It's important that you should believe me,' Moncrieff said moodily. 'I must find somebody who believes me wherever I happen to be. I'm afraid otherwise. It's too lonely. Of course I hurt some people purposely. That dolt Brownlow-Grace for example. I enjoy making him wince. He's been brought up to think life should be considerate to him. His mother, his bank manager, his batman, his bearer – always somebody to mollycoddle him and see to his wants. Christ, the fellow's incapable of wanting anything really. You know he even resents Sister Normanby having to look after other people beside himself. He only considered the war as an opportunity for promotion; I bet he was delighted when Hitler attacked Poland. And there are other people in this world going about with their brains hanging out, their minds half lynched – a fat lot he understands.' He paused, and seeming to catch himself in the middle of his tirade, he laughed softly, 'I was going to write a letter-card to my wife,' he said. 'Still, I haven't got any news. No new love. Next Thursday we'll have some news for them, won't we? I get terribly worked up about this medical board, I can't sleep. You don't think they'll keep me out in India, Weston, do you? It's so lonely out here. I couldn't stay here any longer. I just couldn't.'

'You are in a state, monkey,' Weston said, perturbed and yet laughing, as one cheers a child badly injured. 'Sit quiet a bit, you're speaking loudly. Brownlow'll hear you if you don't take care.'

'Did he?' Moncrieff said suddenly apprehensive. 'He didn't hear me, did he? I don't want to sound as crude as that, even to him.'

'Oh, I don't know. He's not a bad stick,' Weston said. 'He's very sincere and he takes things in good part, even losing his arm, and his career.'

'Oh, I know you can preach a sermon on him easily. I don't think in terms of sermons, that's all,' Moncrieff said. 'But I've been through Burma the same as he has. Why does he sneer at me?' He was silent. Then he said again, 'It's lonely out here.' He sighed. 'I wish I hadn't come out of Burma. I needn't have, I could have let myself go. One night when my leg was gangrenous, the orderly gave me a shot of morphia and I felt myself nodding and smiling. And there was no more jungle, no Japs, no screams, no difficulties at home, no nothing. The orderly would have given me a second shot if I'd asked him. I don't know why

I didn't. It would have finished me off nicely. Say, Weston, have you ever been afraid of Death?'

'I don't think it's as simple as that,' Weston said. 'When I was as good as dead, the first three days here, and for a fortnight afterwards too, I was almost enamoured of death. I'd lost my fear of it. But then I'd lost my will, and my emotions were all dead. I hadn't got any relationships left. It isn't really fair then, is it?'

'I think it is better to fear death,' Moncrieff said slowly. 'Otherwise you grow spiritually proud. With most people it's not so much the fear of death as love of life that keeps them sensible. I don't love life, personally. Only I'm a bit of a coward and I don't want to die again. I loathe Burma, I can't tell you how terribly. I hope they send me home. If you go home, you ought to tell them you got wounded in Burma, you know.'

'Good God, no,' Weston said, outraged. 'Why should I lie?'

'That's all they deserve,' Moncrieff said. 'I wonder what they're doing there now? Talking about reconstruction, I suppose. Even the cinemas will have reconstruction films. Well, maybe I'll get a job in some racket or other. Cramming Sandhurst cadets or something. What will you do when you get home?'

'Moncrieff, my good friend,' Weston said. 'We're soldiers, you know. And it isn't etiquette to talk about going home like that. I'm going in where you left off. I want to have a look at Burma. *And I don't want to see England.*'

'Don't you?' Moncrieff said, ignoring the slow emphasis of Weston's last words and twirling the tassel of his writing-pad slowly. 'Neither do I, very much,' he said with an indifference that ended the conversation.

IV

The sick have their own slightly different world, their jokes are as necessary and peculiar to them as their medicines; they can't afford to be morbid like the healthy, nor to be indifferent to their environment like the Arab. The outside world has been washed out; between them and the encircling mysteries there is only the spotlight of their obsessions holding the small backcloth of ward and garden before them. Anyone appearing before this backcloth has the heightened emphasis and significance of a character upon the stage. The Sikh fortune tellers who offered them promotion and a fortune and England as sibilantly as panders, the mongoose-fight-snake wallahs with their wailing sweet pipes and devitalised cobras, the little native cobblers and peddlers who had customary right to enter the precincts entered as travellers from an unknown land. So did the visitors from the Anglo-India community and brother officers on leave. And each visitor was greedily absorbed and examined by every patient, with the intenser acumen of disease.

Brownlow-Grace had a visitor. This increased his prestige like having a lot of mail. It appeared she had only just discovered he was here, for during the last four days before his medical board she came every day after lunch and stayed sitting on his bed until dusk and conferred upon them an intimacy that evoked in the others a green nostalgia.

She was by any standards a beautiful woman. One afternoon a young unsophisticated English Miss in a fresh little frock and long hair; the next day French and exotic with the pallor of an undertaker's lily and hair like statuary; the third day exquisitely Japanese, carmined and beringed with huge green amber stones, her hair in a high bun that only a great lover would dare unloose. When she left each evening Sister Normanby came in with a great bustle of fresh air and practicality to tidy his bed and put up his mosquito net. And he seemed equally capable of entertaining and being entertained by both ladies.

On the morning of the medical board Brownlow-Grace came and sat by Anthony among the ferns beside the lily pool; and this being a gesture of unusual amiability in one whom training had made rigid, Weston was unreasonably pleased.

'Well, Weston,' he said. 'Sweating on the top line over this medical board?'

'What d'you mean?' Weston asked.

'Well, do you think everything's a wangle to get you home or keep you here like that little squirt Moncrieff?'

'I don't think along those lines, personally,' Weston said. He looked at the long languid officer sprawled in the deck chair. 'The only thing I'm frightened of is that they'll keep me here, or give me some horrible office job where I'll never see a Valentine lift her belly over a bund and go grunting like a wild boar at – well, whoever happens to be there. I got used to the idea of the Germans. I suppose the Japs will do.'

'You're like me; no enemy,' Brownlow-Grace said. 'I didn't think twice about it – till it happened. You're lucky, though. You're the only one of us four who'll ever see action. I could kill some more. What do I want to go home for? They hacked my arm off, those bastards; I blew the fellow's guts out that did it, had the muzzle of my Colt rammed into his belly, I could feel his breath, he was like a frog, the swine. You, I suppose you want to go home, haven't been away long, have you?'

'Six months.'

'Six months without a woman, eh?' Brownlow-Grace laughed, yet kindly.

'Yes.'

'I'm the sort who'll take somebody else's,' Brownlow-Grace said. 'I don't harm them.'

Weston didn't reply.

'You've got a hell of a lot on your mind, haven't you, Weston? Any fool can see something's eating you up.' Still no reply. 'Look here, I may be a fool, but come out with me tonight, let's have a party together. Eh?'

Surprisingly, Weston wasn't embarrassed at this extreme gesture of kindness. It was so ingenuously made. Instead he felt an enormous relief, and for the first time the capacity to speak. Not, he told himself, to ask for advice. Brownlow-Grace wasn't a clergyman with a healing gift; but it was possible to tell him the thing simply, to shift the weight of it a bit. 'I'm all tied up,' he said. 'A party wouldn't be any use, nor a woman.'

'Wouldn't it?' Brownlow-Grace said drily, standing up. Weston had a feeling he was about to go. It would have excruciated him. Instead he half turned, as if to disembarrass him, and said, 'The flowers want watering.'

130

'You know, if you're soldiering, there are some things you've got to put out of bounds to your thoughts,' Weston said. 'Some things you don't let yourself doubt.'

'Your wife, you mean?' Brownlow-Grace said, holding a breath of his cigarette in his lungs and studying the ants on the wall.

'Not only her,' Weston said. 'Look. I didn't start with the same things as you. You had a pram and a private school and saw the sea, maybe. My father was a collier and he worked in a pit. He got rheumatism and nystagmus and then the dole and the parish relief. I'm not telling you a sob story. It's just I was used to different sounds. I used to watch the wheel of the pit spin round year after year, after school and Saturdays and Sundays; and then from 1926 on I watched it not turning round at all, and I can't ever get that wheel out of my mind. It still spins and idles, and there's money and nystagmus coming into the house or no work and worse than nystagmus. I just missed the wheel sucking me down the shaft. I got a scholarship to the county school. I don't know when I started rebelling. Against that wheel in my head. I didn't get along very well. Worked in a grocer's and a printer's, and no job was good enough for me; I had a bug. Plenty of friends too, plenty of chaps thinking the same as me. Used to read books in those days, get passionate about politics, Russia was like a woman to me. Then I did get a job I wanted, in a bookshop in Holborn. A French woman came in one day. I usually talked to customers, mostly politics; but not to her. She came in several times, once with a trade union man I knew. She was short, she had freckles, a straight nose, chestnut hair, she looked about eighteen; she bought books about Beethoven, Schopenhauer, the Renaissance, biology – I read every book she bought, after she'd gone back to France. I asked this chap about her. He said she was a big name, you know the way revolutionary movements toss up a woman sometimes. She was a Communist, big speaker in the industrial towns in North France, she'd been to Russia too. And, well, I just wanted her, more and more and more as the months passed. Not her politics, but her fire. If I could hear her addressing a crowd, never mind about wanting her in those dreams you get.

'And then the war came and most of my friends said it was a phoney war, but I was afraid from the beginning that something would happen to France and I wanted to hear her speaking first. I joined up in November and I made myself such a bloody pest that they posted me to France to reinforcements. I got my war all right. And I met her, too. The trade unionist I told you about gave me a letter to introduce myself. She lived in Lille. She knew me as soon the door opened. And I was just frightened. But after two nights there was no need to be frightened. You get to think for years that life is just a fight, with a flirt thrown in sometimes, a flirt with death or sex or whatever happens to be passing, but mostly a fight all the way along. And then you soften up, you're no use, you haven't got any wheel whirring in your head any more. Only flowers on the table and a piano she plays sometimes, when she wants to, when she wants to love.'

'I've never been to France,' Brownlow-Grace said. 'Hated it at school, French I mean. Communists, of course

– I thought they were all Bolshies, you know, won't obey an order. What happened after Dunkirk?'

'It was such burning sunny weather,' Weston said. 'It was funny, having fine weather. I couldn't get her out of my mind. The sun seemed to expand inside the lining of my brain and the whole fortnight after we made that last stand with Martel at Cambrai I didn't know whether I was looking for her or Dunkirk. When I was most exhausted it was worse, she came to me once by the side of the road, there were several dead Belgian women lying there, and she said "Look, Anthony, I have been raped. They raped me, the Bosche." And the world was crashing and whirring, or it was doped, wouldn't lift a finger to stop it, and the Germans crossing the Seine. A year before I'd have said to the world, "Serve you right." But not now, with Cecile somewhere inside the armies. She'd tried.'

'And that was the end?' Brownlow-Grace said.

'Yes,' said Weston. 'Just about. Only it wasn't a beautiful end, the way it turned out. I had eight months in England, and I never found out a thing. The Free French didn't know. One of them knew her well, knew her as a lover, he told me; boasted about it; I didn't tell him; I wanted to find her, I didn't care about anything else. And then something started in me. I used to mooch about London. A French girl touched me on the street one night. I went with her. I went with a lot of women. Then we embarked for overseas. I had a girl at Durban, and in Bombay: sometimes they were French, if possible they were French. God, it was foul.'

He got up and sat on the edge of the pool; under the

green strata of mosses the scaled goldfish moved slowly in their palaces of burning gold. He wiped his face which was sweating.

'Five days ago I got this letter from America,' he said. 'From her.'

Brownlow-Grace said, 'That was a bit of luck.' Weston laughed.

'Yes,' he said. 'Yes. It was nice of her to write. She put it very nicely, too. Would you like to read it?'

'No,' said Brownlow-Grace. 'I don't want to read it.'

'She said it often entered her mind to write to me, because I had been so sweet to her, in Lille, that time. She hoped I was well. To enter America there had been certain formalities, she said; she'd married an American, a country which has all types, she said. There is a Life, she said, but not mine, and a war also, but not mine. Now it is the Japanese. That's all she said.'

'She remembered you,' Brownlow-Grace said.

'Some things stick in a woman's mind,' Weston said. 'She darned my socks for me in bed. Why didn't she say she remembered darning my socks?'

Brownlow-Grace pressed his hand, fingers extended, upon the surface of the water, not breaking its resistance, quite.

'I don't use the word,' he said. 'But I guess it's because she loved you.'

Weston looked up, searching and somehow naïve.

'I don't mind about the Japanese,' he said, 'if that were so.'

V

Dad Withers had his medical board first; he wasn't in the board room long; in fact he was back on the verandah outside 'O' 3 (b) when Weston returned from sending a cable at the camp post office.

'Did it go all right, Dad?' Weston asked.

'Sure, sure,' Dad said, purring as if at his own cleverness. 'Three colonels and two majors there, and the full colonel he said to me, "Well, Withers, what's your trouble? Lieutenant-Quartermaster, weren't you?" And I said, "Correct, sir, and now I'm putting my own body in for exchange, sir. It don't keep the rain out no more, sir." So he said, "You're not much use to us, Withers, by the look of you." And I said, "Not a bit of use, sir, sorry to report." And the end of it was they give me a free berth on the next ship home wiv full military honours and a disability pension and all. Good going, isn't it now?'

'Very good, Dad. I'm very pleased.'

'Thank you,' Dad said, his face wrinkled and benign as a tortoise. 'Now go and get your own ticket and don't keep the gentlemen waiting...'

Dad lay half asleep in the deck chair, thinking that it was all buttoned up now, all laid on, all made good. It had been a long time, a lifetime, more than twenty hot seasons, more than twenty rains. Not many could say that. Not many had stuck it like him. Five years in Jhansi with his body red as lobster from head to toe with prickly heat, squirting a water pistol down his back for enjoyment and scratching his shoulders with a long fork from the bazaar. Two big wars there'd been, and most of the boys had been glad to go into them, excited to be posted to France, or embark for Egypt. But he'd stuck it out. Still here, still good for a game of nap, and them all dead, the boys that wanted to get away. And now it was finished with him, too.

He didn't know. Maybe he wasn't going home the way he'd figured it out after all. Maybe there was something else, something he hadn't counted in. This tiredness, this emptiness, this grey blank wall of mist, this not caring. What would it be like in the small Council house with five youngsters and his missus? She'd changed a lot, the last photo she sent she was like his mother, spectacles and fat legs, full of plainness. Maybe the kids would play with him, though, the two young ones?

He pulled himself slowly out of his seat, took out his wallet, counted his money; ninety chips he had. Enough to see India just once again. Poor old India. He dressed hurriedly, combed his thin hair, wiped his spectacles, dusted his shoes and left before the others came back. He picked up a tonga at the stand outside the main gates of the hospital cantonment, just past the M.D. lines, and named a certain hotel down town. And off he cantered, the skinny old horse clattering and letting off great puffs of bad air under the tonga wallah's whip, and Dad shouting, 'Jillo, jillo,' impatient to be drunk.

Brownlow-Grace came in and went straight to the little bed table where he kept his papers in an untidy heap. He went there in a leisurely way, avoiding the inquiring silences of Weston and Moncrieff and Sister Normanby, who were all apparently doing something. He fished out an airgraph form and his fountain-pen and sat quietly on the edge of his bed.

'Oh damn and blast it,' he said angrily. 'My pen's dry.'

Weston gave him an inkbottle.

He sat down again.

'What's the date?' he said after a minute.

'12th,' Moncrieff said.

'What month?' he asked.

'December.'

'Thanks.'

He wrote slowly, laboriously, long pauses between sentences. When he finished he put his pen away and looked for a stamp.

'What stamp d'you put on an airgraph?' he said.

'Three annas,' Moncrieff said patiently.

Sister Normanby decided to abolish the embarrassing reticence with which this odd man was concealing his board result. She had no room for broody hens.

'Well,' she said, gently enough. 'What happened at the board?'

He looked up at her and neither smiled nor showed any sign of recognition. Then he stood up, took his cane and peaked service cap, and brushed a speck of down off his long and well-fitting trousers.

'They discharged me,' he said. 'Will you post this airgraph for me, please?'

'Yes,' she said, and for some odd reason she found herself unable to deal with the situation and took it from him and went on with her work.

'I'm going out,' he said.

Weston followed him into the garden and caught him up by the lily pool.

'Is that invitation still open?' he asked.

'What invitation?' Brownlow-Grace said.

'To go on the spree with you tonight?' Weston said.

Brownlow-Grace looked at him thoughtfully.

'I've changed my mind, Anthony,' he said – Weston was pleasurably aware of this first use of his Christian name – 'I don't think I'd be any use to you tonight. Matter of fact, I phoned Rita just now, you know the woman who comes to see me, and she's calling for me in five minutes.'

'I see,' Weston said. 'OK by me.'

'You don't mind, do you?' he said. 'I don't think you need Rita's company, do you? Besides, she usually prefers one man at a time. She's the widow of a friend of mine, Mostyn Turner; he was killed in Burma, too.'

Weston came back into the ward to meet Sister Normanby's white face. 'Where's he gone?' she said.

Weston looked at her, surprised at the emotion and stress this normally imperturbable woman was showing.

He didn't answer her.

'He's gone to that woman,' she said, white and virulent. 'Hasn't he?'

'Yes, he has,' he said quietly.

'She always has them when they're convalescent,' she said, flashing with venom. She picked up her medicine book and the jar with her thermometer in it. 'I have them when they're sick.'

She left the ward, biting her white lips.

'I didn't know she felt that way about him,' Weston said.

'Neither did she,' said Moncrieff. 'She never knows till it's too late. That's the beauty about her. She's virginal.'

'You're very cruel, Moncrieff.'

Moncrieff turned on him like an animal.

'Cruel?' he said. 'Cruel? Well, I don't lick Lazarus' sores, Weston. I take the world the way it is. Nobody cares about you out here. Nobody. What have I done to anybody? Why should they keep me here? What's the use of keeping a man with infantile paralysis and six inches of bone missing from his leg? Why didn't the board let me go home?'

'You'll go home, monkey, you'll go home,' Weston said gently. 'You know the Army. You can help them out here. You're bound to go home, when the war ends.'

'Do you think so?' Moncrieff said. 'Do you?' He thought of this for a minute at least. Then he said, 'No, I shall never go home. I know it.'

'Don't be silly, monkey. You're a bit run down, that's all.' Weston soothed him. 'Let's go and sit by the pool for a while.'

'I like the pool,' Moncrieff said. They strolled out together and sat on the circular ledge. The curving bright branches held their leaves peacefully above the water. Under the mosses they could see the old toad of the pond sleeping, his back rusty with jewels. Weston put his hand in the water; minnows rose in small flocks and nibbled at his fingers. Circles of water lapped softly outwards, outwards, till they touched the edge of the pool, and cast a gentle wetness on the stone, and lapped again inwards, inwards. And as they lapped inwards he felt the ripples surging against the most withdrawn and inmost ledges of his being,

139

like a series of temptations in the wilderness. And he felt glad tonight, feeling some small salient gained when for many reasons the men whom he was with were losing ground along the whole front to the darkness that there is.

'No,' said Moncrieff at last. 'Talking is no good. But perhaps you will write to me sometimes, will you, just to let me know.'

'Yes, I'll write to you, monkey,' Weston said, looking up.

And then he looked away again, not willing to consider those empty inarticulate eyes.

'The mosquitoes are starting to bite,' he said. 'We'd better go now.'

THE ORANGE GROVE

The grey truck slowed down at the crossroads and the Army officer leaned out to read the signpost. *Indians Only*, the sign pointing to the native town read. *Dak Bungalow* straight on. 'Thank God,' said Staff-Captain Beale. 'Go ahead, driver.' They were lucky hitting a dak bungalow at dusk. They'd bivouacked the last two nights, and in the monsoon a bivouac is bad business. Tonight they'd be able to strip and sleep dry under a roof, and heat up some bully on the Tommy cooker. Bloody good.

These bungalows are scattered all over India on the endless roads and travellers may sleep there, cook their food, and pass on. The rooms are bare and whitewashed, the verandah has room for a camp bed, they are quiet and remote, tended for the Government only by some old khansama or chowkey, usually a slippered and silent old

143

Moslem. The driver pulled in and began unpacking the kit, the dry rations, the cooker, the camp bed, his blanket roll, the tin of kerosene. Beale went off to find the caretaker, whom he discovered squatting amongst the flies by the well. He was a wizened yellow-skinned old man in a soiled dhoti. Across his left breast was a plaster, loose and dripping with pus, a permanent discharge it seemed. He wheezed as he replied to the brusque request and raised himself with pain, searching slowly for his keys.

Beale came to give the driver a hand while the old man fumbled with the crockery indoors.

'The old crow is only sparking on one cylinder,' he said. 'Looks like TB,' he added with the faint overtone of disgust which the young and healthy feel for all incurable diseases. He looked out at the falling evening, the fulgurous inflammation among the grey anchorages of cloud, the hot creeping prescience of the monsoon.

'I don't like it tonight,' he said. 'It's eerie; I can't breathe or think. This journey's getting on my nerves. What day is it? I've lost count.'

'Thursday, sir,' the driver said, 'August 25.'

'How do you know all that?' Beale asked, curious.

'I have been thinking it out, for to write a letter tonight,' the driver said. 'Shall I get the cooker going, sir? Your bed is all ready now.'

'OK,' Beale said, sitting on his camp bed and opening his grip. He took out a leather writing-pad in which he kept the notes he was making for Divisional HQ, and all the letters he'd received from home. He began looking among the letters for one he wanted. The little dusty driver tinkered with the cooker. Sometimes Beale looked up and watched him, sometimes he looked away at the night.

This place seemed quiet enough. The old man had warned him there was unrest and rioting in the town. The lines had been cut, the oil tanks unsuccessfully attacked, the court house burnt down, the police had made lathi charges, the district magistrate was afraid to leave his bungalow. The old man had relished the violence of others. Of course you couldn't expect the 11th to go by without some riots, some deaths. Even in this remote part of Central India where the native princes ruled from their crumbling Mogul forts through their garrisons of smiling crop-headed little Ghurkas. But it seemed quiet enough here, a mile out of the town. The only chance was that someone might have seen them at the cross roads; it was so sultry, so swollen and angry, the sky, the hour. He felt for his revolver.

He threw the driver a dry box of matches from his grip. Everything they carried was fungoid with damp, the driver had been striking match after match on his wet box with a curious depressive impassivity. Funny little chap, seemed to have no initiative, as if some part of his will were paralysed. Maybe it was that wife of his he'd talked about the night before last when they had the wood fire going in the hollow. Funny, Beale had been dazed with sleep, half listening, comprehending only the surface of the slow, clumsy words. Hate. Hate. Beale couldn't understand hate. War hadn't taught it to him, war was to him only fitness, discomfort, feats of endurance, proud muscles, a career, irresponsible dissipation, months of austerity broken by 'blinds' in Cairo, or Durban, Calcutta or Bangalore or Bombay. But this little rough-head with his soiled hands and bitten nails, his odd blue eyes looking away, his mean bearing, squatting on the floor with kerosene and grease over his denims – he had plenty of hate.

'...tried to emigrate first of all, didn't want to stay anywhere. I was fourteen, finished with reformatory schools for keeps... New Zealand I wanted to go. There was a school in Bristol for emigrants... I ran away from home but they didn't bother with me in Bristol, nacherly... Police sent me back. So then I become a boy in the Army, in the drums, and then I signed on. I'm a time-serving man, sir; better put another couple of branches on the fire; so I went to Palestine, against the Arabs; seen them collective farms the Jews got there, sir? Oranges... then I come home, so I goes on leave... We got a pub in our family and since my father died my mother been keeping it... for the colliers it is... never touch beer myself, my father boozed himself to death be'ind the counter. Well, my mother 'ad a barmaid, a flash dame she was, she was good for trade, fit for an answer any time, and showing a bit of her breasts every time she drew a pint. Red hair she had, well not exactly red, I don't know the word, not so *coarse* as red. My mother said for me to keep off her. My mother is a big Bible woman, though nacherly she couldn't go to chapel down our way being she kept a pub... Well, Monica, this barmaid, she slept in the attic, it's a big 'ouse, the Bute's Arms. And I was nineteen. You can't always answer for yourself, can you? It was my pub by rights, *mine*. She was *my* barmaid. That's how my father'd have said if he wasn't

146

dead. My mother wouldn't have no barmaids when he was alive. Monica knew what she was doing all right. She wanted the pub and the big double bed; she couldn't wait... It didn't seem much to pay for sleeping with a woman like that... Well, then I went back to barracks, and it wasn't till I told my mate and he called me a sucker that I knew I couldn't... Nothing went right after that. She took good care to get pregnant, Monica did, and my mother threw her out. But it was my baby, and I married her without telling my mother. It was *my* affair, wasn't it? *Mine.*'

How long he had been telling all this Beale couldn't remember. There was nothing to pin that evening upon; the fire and the logs drying beside the fire, the circle of crickets, the sudden blundering of moths into the warm zone of the fire and thoughtful faces, the myopic sleepy stare of fatigue, and those bitter distasteful words within intervals of thought and waiting. Not until now did Beale realise that there had been no hard-luck story told, no gambit for sympathy or compassionate leave or a poor person's divorce. But a man talking into a wood fire in the remote asylums of distance, and slowly explaining the twisted and evil curvature of his being.

'She told me she'd get her own back on me for my mother turning her out... And she did... I know a man in my own regiment that slept with her on leave. But the kid is mine. My mother got the kid for me. She shan't spoil the kid. Nobody'll spoil the kid, neither Monica nor me... I can't make it out, how is it a woman is so wonderful, I mean in a bedroom? I should 'a' murdered her, it would be better than this, this hating her all the time. Wouldn't it?...'

'The Tommy cooker's OK now, sir,' the driver said. 'The wind was blowing the flame back all the time. OK now with this screen. What's it to be? There's only bully left.'

'Eh? What?' Beale said. 'Oh, supper? Bully? I can't eat any more bully. Can't we get some eggs or something? Ten days with bully twice a day is plenty. Can you eat bully?'

'Can't say I fancy it,' the driver said. 'I'll go down the road and see if I can get some eggs.'

'I shouldn't bother,' Beale said. 'The storm will get you if you go far. Besides, it's dangerous down the town road. They've been rioting since Gandhi and Nehru were arrested last week. Better brew up and forget about the food.'

Beale was by nature and by his job as a staff officer one who is always doing things and forgetting about them. It was convenient as well as necessary to him. His *Pending* basket was always empty. He never had a load on his mind.

'I'll take a walk just the same,' the driver said. 'Maybe I'll find a chicken laying on the road. I won't be long.'

He was a good scrounger, it was a matter of pride with him to get anything that was wanted, mosquito poles, or water or anything. And every night, whether they were in the forest or the desert plains that encompass Indore, he had announced his intention of walking down the road.

Some impulse caused Beale to delay him a moment.

'Remember,' Beale said, 'the other night, you said you saw the collective farms in Palestine?'

'Aye,' said the driver, standing in the huge deformity of the hunch-backed shadow that the lamp projected from his slovenly head.

'They were good places, those farms?' Beale asked.

'Aye, they were,' the driver said, steadying his childish gaze. 'They didn't have money, they didn't buy and sell. They shared what they had and the doctor and the school teacher the same as the labourer or the children, all the same, all living together. Orange groves they lived in, and I would like to go back there.'

He stepped down from the porch and the enormous shadows vanished from the roof and from the wall. Beale sat on, the biscuit tin of water warming slowly on the cooker, the flying ants casting their wings upon the glass of the lamp and the sheets of his bed. An orange grove in Palestine... He was experiencing one of those enlargements of the imagination that come once or perhaps twice to a man, and recreate him subtly and profoundly. And he was thinking simply this – that some things are possible and other things are impossible to us. Beyond the mass of vivid and sensuous impressions which he had allowed the war to impose upon him were the quiet categories of the possible and the quieter frozen infinities of the impossible. And he must get back to those certainties... The night falls, and the dance bands turn on the heat. The indolent arrive in their taxis, the popsies and the good-timers, the lonely good-looking boys and the indifferent erotic women. Swing music sways across the bay from the urbane permissive ballrooms of the Taj and Green's. *In the Mood*, *It's foolish but it's fun*, some doughboys cracking whips in the coffee-room, among apprehensive glances, the taxi drivers buy a betel leaf and spit red saliva over the running-board, and panders touch the sleeves of the soldiers, the crowd huddles beneath the Gateway, turning up collars and umbrellas everywhere against the thin sane arrows of the rain. And who is she whose song is the world spinning, whose lambent streams cast their curved ways about you and about, whose languors are the infinite desires of the unknowing? Is she the girl behind the grille, in the side street where they play gramophone records and you pay ten chips for a whisky and you suddenly feel a godalmighty yen for whoever it is in your arms? But beyond that? Why had he failed with this woman, why had it been impossible with that woman? He collected the swirl of thought and knew that he could not generalise as the driver had done in the glow of the wood fire. Woman. The gardener at the boarding school he went to used to say things about women. Turvey his name was. Turvey, the headmaster called him, but the boys had to say *Mr* Turvey. Mr Turvey didn't hold with mixed bathing, not at any price, because woman wasn't clean like man, he said. And when the boys demurred, thinking of soft pledges and film stars and the moon, Mr Turvey would wrinkle his saturnine face and say, 'Course you young gentlemen knows better than me. I only been married fifteen years. I don't know nothing of course.' And maybe this conversation would be while he was emptying the ordure from the latrines into the oil drum on iron wheels which he trundled each morning down to his sewer pits in the school gardens.

But in an intenser lucidity Beale knew he must not generalise. There would be perhaps one woman out of many, one life out of many, two things possible – if life itself were possible, and if he had not debased himself among the impossibilities by then. The orange grove in Palestine...

And then he realised that the water in the biscuit tin was boiling and he knelt to put the tea and tinned milk into the two enamel mugs. As he knelt a drop of rain the size of a coin pitted his back. And another. And a third. He shuddered. Ten days they'd been on the road, making this reconnaissance for a projected Army exercise, and each day had been nothing but speed and distance hollow in the head, the mileometer ticking up the daily two hundred, the dust of a hundred villages justifying their weariness with its ashes, and tomorrow also only speed and distance and the steadiness of the six cylinders. And he'd been dreaming of a Bombay whore whose red kiss he still had not washed from his arm, allowing her to enter where she would and push into oblivion the few things that were possible to him in the war and the peace. And now the rain made him shudder and he felt all the loneliness of India about him and he knew he had never been more alone. So he was content to watch the storm gather, operating against him from a heavy fulcrum in the east, lashing the bungalow and the trees, infuriating the night. The cooker spluttered and went out. He made no move to use the boiling water upon the tea. The moths flew in from the rain, and the grasshoppers and the bees. The frogs grunted and croaked in the swirling mud and grass, the night was animate and violent. He waited without moving until the violence of the storm was spent. Then he looked at his watch. It was, as he thought. The driver had been gone an hour and twenty minutes. He knew he must go and look for him.

He loaded his revolver carefully and buckled on his holster over his bush shirt. He called for the old caretaker, but there was no reply. The bungalow was empty. He turned down the wick of the lamp and putting on his cap, stepped softly into the night. It was easy to get lost. It would be difficult to find anything tonight, unless it was plumb in the main road.

His feet felt under the streaming water for the stones of the road. The banyan tree he remembered, it was just beyond the pull-in. Its mass was over him now, he could feel it over his head. It was going to be difficult. The nearest cantonment was four hundred miles away; in any case the roads were too flooded now for him to retrace his way to Mhow. If he went on to Baroda, Ahmedabad – but the Mahi river would be in spate also. The lines down everywhere, too. They would have to go on, that he felt sure about. Before daybreak, too. It wasn't safe here. If only he could find the driver. He was irritated with the driver, irritated in a huge cloudy way, for bungling yet one more thing, for leaving him alone with so much on his hands, for insisting on looking for eggs. He'd known something would happen.

He felt the driver with his foot and knelt down over him in the swirling road and felt for his heart under his sodden shirt and cursed him in irritation and concern. Dead as a duckboard, knifed. The rain came on again and he tried to lift up the corpse the way he'd been taught, turning it first on to its back and standing firmly astride it. But the driver was obstinate and heavy and for a long time he refused to be lifted up.

He carried the deadweight back up the road, sweating and bitched by the awkward corpse, stumbling and trying in vain to straighten himself. What a bloody mess, he kept saying; I told him not to go and get eggs; did he have to have eggs for supper? It became a struggle between himself and the corpse, who was trying to slide down off his back and stay lying on the road. He had half a mind to let it have its way.

He got back eventually and backed himself against the verandah like a lorry, letting the body slide off his back; the head fell crack against the side wall and he said 'Sorry,' and put a sack between the cheek and the ground. The kid was soaking wet and wet red mud in his hair; he wiped his face up with cotton-waste and put a blanket over him while he packed the kit up and stowed it in the truck. He noticed the tea and sugar in the mugs and tried the temper of the water. It was too cold. He regretted it. He had the truck packed by the end of half an hour, his own bedding roll stretched on top of the baggage ready for the passenger. He hoped he'd be agreeable this time. He resisted a bit but he had stiffened a little and was more manageable. He backed him into the truck and then climbed in, pulling him on to the blankets by his armpits. Not until he'd put up the tailboard and got him all ready did he feel any ease. He sighed. They were away. He got into the driving seat to switch on the ignition. Then he realised there was no key. He felt a momentary panic. But surely the driver had it. He slipped out and, in the darkness and the drive of the rain, searched in the man's pockets. Paybook, matches, identity discs (must remember that, didn't even know his name), at last the keys.

He started the engine and let her warm up, slipped her into second, and drove slowly out. The old caretaker never appeared, and Beale wondered whether he should say anything of his suspicions regarding the old man when he made his report. Unfortunately there was no evidence. Still, they were away from there; he sighed with relief as the compulsion under which he had been acting relaxed. He had this extra sense, of which he was proud, of being able to feel the imminence of danger as others feel a change in the weather; it didn't help him in Libya, perhaps it hindered him there; but in a pub in Durban it had got him out in the nick of time; he'd edged for the door before a shot was fired. He knew tonight all right. The moment he saw that dull red lever of storm raised over his head, and the old caretaker had shrugged his shoulders after his warning had been laughed off. You had to bluff them; only sometimes bluff wasn't enough and then you had to get away, face or no face. Now he tried to remember the route on the map; driving blind, the best thing was to go slow and pull in somewhere a few miles on. Maybe the sun would rise sometime and he could dry out the map and work out the best route; no more native towns for him; he wanted to get to a cantonment if possible. Otherwise he'd look for the police lines at Dohad or Jabhua or wherever the next place was. But every time he thought of pulling in, a disinclination to stop the engine made him keep his drenched ammunition boot on the accelerator pedal. When he came to a road junction he followed his fancy; there is such a thing as letting the car do the guiding.

He drove for six hours before the night stirred at all. Then his red-veined eyes felt the slight lessening in the effectiveness of the headlights that presaged the day. When he could see the red berm of the road and the flooded paddy-fields lapping the bank, he at last pulled up under a tree and composed himself over the wheel, placing his cheek against the rim, avoiding the horn at the centre. He fell at once into a stiff rigid sleep.

A tribe of straggling gypsies passed him soon after dawn. They made no sound, leading their mules and camels along the soft berm on the other side of the road, mixing their own ways with no other's. The sun lay back of the blue rain-clouds, making the earth steam. The toads hopped out of the mud and rested under the stationary truck. Land-crabs came out of the earth and sat on the edge of their holes. Otherwise no one passed. The earth seemed content to let him have his sleep out. He woke about noon, touched by the sun as it passed.

He felt guilty. Guilty of neglect of duty, having slept at his post? Then he got a grip on himself and rationalised the dreadful guilt away. What could he have done about it? The driver had been murdered. What did they expect him to do? Stay there and give them a second treat? Stay there and investigate? Or get on and report it. Why hadn't he reported it earlier? How could he? The lines were down, the roads flooded behind him, he was trying his best; he couldn't help sleeping for a couple of hours. Yet the guilt complex persisted. It was a bad dream and he had some evil in him, a soft lump of evil in his brain. But why? If he'd told the man to go for eggs it would be different. He was bound to be all right as long as he had his facts right. Was there an accident report to be filled in immediately, in duplicate, Army Form B– something-or-other? He took out his notebook, but the paper was too wet to take his hard pencil. 23.00 hrs. on 23 August 1942 deceased stated his desire to get some eggs. I warned him that disturbances of a political character had occurred in the area... He shook himself, bleary and sore-throated, in his musty overalls, and thought a shave and some food would put him right. He went round to the back of the truck. The body had slipped with the jolting of the road. He climbed in and looked at the ashen face. The eyes were closed, the face had sunk into an expressionless inanition, it made him feel indifferent to the whole thing. Poor sod. Where was his hate now? Was he grieving that the woman, Mona was it, would get a pension out of him now? Did he still hate her? He seemed to have let the whole matter drop. Death was something without hate in it. But he didn't want to do anything himself except shave and eat and get the whole thing buttoned up. He tore himself away from the closed soiled face and ferreted about for his shaving kit. He found it at last, and after shaving in the muddy rain-water he ate a few hard biscuits and stuffed a few more into his pocket. Then he lashed the canvas down over the tailboard and got back to the wheel. The truck was slow to start. The bonnet had been leaking and the plugs were wet in the cylinder heads. She wouldn't spark for a minute or two. Anxiety swept over him. He cursed the truck viciously. Then she sparked on a couple of cylinders, stuttered for a minute as the others dried out, and settled down steadily. He ran her away carefully and again relaxed. He was dead scared of being stranded with the body. There wasn't even a shovel on the truck.

After driving for an hour he realised he didn't know where he was. He was in the centre of a vast plain of paddy-fields, lined by raised bunds and hedged with cactus along the road. White herons and tall fantastic cranes stood by the pools in the hollows. He pulled up to try and work out his position. But his map was nowhere to be found. He must have left it at the dak bungalow in his haste. He looked at his watch; it had stopped. Something caved in inside him, a sensation of panic, of an enemy against whose machinations he had failed to take the most elementary precautions. He was lost.

He moved on again at once. There was distance. The mileometer still measured something? By sunset he would do so many miles. How much of the day was left? Without the sun how could he tell? He was panicky at not knowing these things; he scarcely knew more than the man in the back of the truck. So he drove on and on, passing nobody but a tribe of gypsies with their mules and camels, and dark peasants driving their bullocks knee-deep in the alluvial mud before their simple wooden ploughs. He drove as fast as the track would allow; in some places it was flooded and narrow, descending to narrow causeways swept by brown streams which he only just managed to cross. He drove till the land was green with evening, and in the crepuscular uncertainty he halted and decided to kip

down for the night. He would need petrol; it was kept in
tins in the back of the truck; it meant pulling the body out,
or making him sit away in a corner. He didn't want to
disturb the kid. He'd been jolted all day; and now this
indignity. He did all he had to do with a humility that was
alien to him. Respect he knew; but this was more than
respect; obedience and necessity he knew, but this was
more than either of these. It was somehow an admission of
the integrity of the man, a new interest in what he was and
what he had left behind. He got some soap and a towel,
after filling his tanks, and when he had washed himself he
propped the driver up against the tailboard and sponged
him clean and put P.T. shoes on his feet instead of the boots
that had so swollen his feet. When he had laid him out on
the blankets and covered him with a sheet, he rested from
his exertions, and as he recovered his breath he glanced
covertly at him, satisfied that he had done something for
him. What would the woman have done, Monica? Would
she have flirted with him? Most women did, and he didn't
discourage them. But this woman, my God, he'd bloody
well beat her up. It was her doing, this miserable end, this
mess-up. He hadn't gone down the road to get eggs; he'd
gone to get away from her. It must have been a habit of his,
at nights, to compose himself. She'd bitched it all. He could
just see her. And she still didn't know a thing about him,
not the first thing. Yes, he hated her all right, the
voluptuous bitch.

He slept at the wheel again, falling asleep with a biscuit
still half chewed in his mouth. He had erotic dreams, this
woman Monica drawing him a pint, and her mouth and her

breasts and the shallow taunting eyes; and the lights in her attic bedroom with the door ajar, and the wooden stairs creaking. And the dawn then laid its grey fingers upon him and he woke with the same feeling of guilt and shame, a grovelling debased mood, that had seized him the first morning. He got up, stretching himself, heady with vertigo and phlegm, and washed himself in the paddy flood. He went round to the back of the truck to get some biscuits. He got them quietly, the boy was still sleeping, and he said to himself that he would get him through today, honest he would. He had to.

The sun came out and the sky showed a young summer blue. The trees wakened and shook soft showers of rain off their leaves. Hills showed blue as lavender and when he came to the cross-roads he steered north-west by the sun, reckoning to make the coast road somewhere near Baroda. There would be a cantonment not far from there, and a Service dump for coffins, and someone to whom he could make a report. It would be an immense relief. His spirits rose. Driving was tricky; the worn treads of the tyres tended to skid, the road wound up and down the ghats, through tall loose scrub, but he did not miss seeing the shy jungle wanderers moving through the bush with their bows, tall lithe men like fauns with black hair over their eyes that were like grapes. They would stand a moment under a tree, and glide away back into the bush. There were villages now, and women of light olive skin beating their saris on the stones, rhythmically, and their breasts uncovered.

And then, just when he felt he was out of the lost zones, in the late afternoon, he came down a long sandy track through cactus to a deep and wide river at which the road ended. A gypsy tribe was fording it and he watched them to gauge the depth of the river. The little mules, demure as mice, kicked up against the current, nostrils too near the water to neigh; the camels followed the halter, stately as bishops, picking their calm way. The babies sat on their parents' heads, the women unwound their saris and put them in a bundle on their crowns, the water touched their breasts. And Beale pushed his truck into bottom gear and nosed her cautiously into the stream. Midway across the brown tide swept up to his sparking plugs and the engine stopped. He knew at once that he was done for. The river came up in waves over the sideboards and his whole concern was that the boy inside would be getting wet. A gypsy waded past impersonally, leading two bright-eyed grey mules. Beale hailed him. He nodded and went on. Beale called out 'Help!' The gypsies gathered on the far bank and discussed it. He waved and eventually three of them came wading out to him. He knew he must abandon the truck till a recovery section could be sent out to salvage it, but he must take his companion with him, naturally. When the gypsies reached him he pointed to the back of the truck, unlaced the tarpaulin and showed them the corpse. They nodded their heads gravely. Their faces were serious and hard. He contrived to show them what he wanted and when he climbed in they helped him intelligently to hoist the body out. They contrived to get it on to their heads, ducking down under the tailboard till their faces were submerged in the scum of the flood.

They carried him ashore that way, Beale following with his revolver and webbing. They held a conclave on the sand while the women wrung out their saris and the children crowded round the body. Beale stood in the centre of these lean outlandish men, not understanding a word. They talked excitedly, abruptly, looking at him and at the corpse. He fished his wallet out of his pocket and showed them a five-rupee note. He pointed to the track and to the mules. They nodded and came to some domestic agreement. One of them led a little mule down to the stream and they strapped a board across its bony moulting back, covering the board with sacking. Four of them lifted the body up and lashed it along the spar. Then they smiled at Beale, obviously asking for his approval of their skill. He nodded back and said, 'That's fine.' The gypsies laid their panniers on the mules, the women wound their saris about their swarthy bodies, called their children, formed behind their men. The muleteer grinned and nodded his head to Beale. The caravanserai went forward across the sands. Beale turned back once to look at the truck, but he was too bloody tired and fed up to mind. It would stay there; it was settled in; if the floods rose it would disappear; if they fell so much the better. He couldn't help making a balls of it all. He had the body, that was one proof; they could find the truck if they came to look for it, that was the second proof. If they wanted an accident report they could wait. If they thought he was puddled they could sack him when they liked. What was it all about, anyway?

Stumbling up the track in the half-light among the ragged garish gypsies he gradually lost the stiff self-consciousness with which he had first approached them. He was thinking of a page near the beginning of a history book he had studied in the Sixth at school in 1939. About the barbarian migrations in pre-history; the Celts and Iberians, Goths and Vandals and Huns. Once Life had been nothing worth recording beyond the movements of people like these, camels and asses piled with the poor property of their days, panniers, rags, rope, gramm and dahl, lambs and kids too new to walk, barefooted, long-haired people rank with sweat, animals shivering with ticks, old women striving to keep up with the rest of the family. He kept away from the labouring old women, preferring the tall girls who walked under the primitive smooth heads of the camels. He kept his eye on the corpse, but he seemed comfortable enough. Except he was beginning to corrupt.

There was a faint whiff of badness about him... What did the gypsies do? They would burn him, perhaps, if the journey took too long. How many days to Baroda? The muleteer nodded his head and grinned.

Well, as long as he had the man's identity discs and paybook, he would be covered. He must have those... He slipped the identity discs over the wet blue head and matted hair and put them in his overall pocket. He would be all right now, even if they burned him... It would be a bigger fire than the one they had sat by and fed with twigs and talked about women together that night, how many nights ago?

He wished, though, that he knew where they were going. They only smiled and nodded when he asked. Maybe they weren't going anywhere much, except perhaps to some pasture, to some well.

THE REUNION

In the afternoon the sun uncurls his sting as a scorpion its tail. Like the scorpion the sun is animate and animal and vicious, making for his habitat stones and dust. Out of the stones and dust here, now, emerge slowly roads, pavements, bazaar, hotels, railway station, car park, canteens, cinemas. Before crumbling under the uncurling tail of the sun they poise, pause for a century, containing people. Contain people who emerge, pirouette, incredible palaver and goings-on, poise, pause, revert. The hotel is in the middle of the town, at the crossroads, walled in, a taxi rank at its doors. Central, convenient, slovenly. British officers and white women lunching, damp fish, cold gravy on red beef, soiled white of the waiters, their bare feet stirring the dust. The rice was boiled to death today, the curry is watery, fetch the manager at once. The sweeper drives the fag-ends before him slowly with twig brush, bending dustily. The chowkeydar contemplates the shade with green eyes, the room boys lie on the inner pavement, smoking brown leaf, spitting red betel juice, eyes indolent with submerging consciousness. The violence of the sun makes inertia ominous. There must be violence, curled in the cracked stones perhaps, to sleep to dream, aye there's the rub. Like a jackdaw a child swoops on the shaking of table cloths and seizes a crust to allay the hardness in its shrunken belly. The beggar women, old timers, infamous, Lazarene, pester the emerging guests, bakshish, bakshish, rajah sahib, their bellies drawn tight as though with worry. A tonga driver becomes vociferous, demands more than the soldier will give, snatches, is pushed away. At noon an altercation, at night a fight, a knife. Wealth retires to its rooms, the high rank, the red tabs, the civil servant in lounge suit, the bourgeois with an emergency commission, sleep tickles them, washes out the sandpaper quality of their bustle, the hardness of their dubious currency. For two hours money withdraws itself from circulation.

Obviously brothers, the eyes at the tables said, considering the saturnine boyish faces of the two chatting amid close and tranquil silences, exchanging snaps and air letter-cards, smiling slowly, unaware of the eyes. Both boys, the one a captain with a limp, a loose mouth, devastating darling, so sulky, simply divine, I wonder who: the other raw, hair strong and ungroomed, little almond eyes, broad cheekbones, such very thick eyebrows, hunched shoulders, funny little private soldier, of course they say in England private soldiers can go anywhere,

166

simply anywhere, Savoy, Berkeley – obviously brothers, that explains how it is. Sweet, rather. In the canteen, when one has to, sometimes some of them are really rather, you can't help but... but how nice for their mother to think, brothers together today.

'I didn't think I'd see any of the family again.'

'What? Never again?'

'Maybe.'

'You mustn't say that, kid.'

'Only to you.'

'Did you want to?'

'What? See you or Eunice or Mums again? I should say.'

'I got so I didn't want to.'

'But that's very bad for you.'

'Oh yes, I know.'

'What shall we do this afternoon?'

'Don't mind.'

'Neither do I. Let's not do it, then.'

'What?'

'Whatever we were going to do. Did you have a rough voyage? Was Durban OK?'

'The ship was terrible. For us. The officers were all right. Cabins, and a smashing dining saloon, menus in French; I saw them because we used to have Urdu classes in the saloon. What French! Petits pois Navarre, potage Henri Quatre. The barber's shop had a notice, "Out Of Bounds To Third Class Passengers. Third Class Passengers May Make Purchases Through The Porthole." The sea was lovely, though, and the stars. I slept on deck as soon as the sea turned blue.'

'Yes, I know.'

'The troop train was the next thing. It was waiting for us at Ballard Pier. Six days of it. No fans, wooden racks. I had a whole rack. There was a man wouldn't take off his boots for four days. We were on to him all the time. When he did take them off we made him put them on again till we got to a platform. You don't notice another smell on a platform.'

'You had it raw.'

'We had it tinned. Bully and biscuits for six days. If it had been an electric train we'd have had no tea, either. I enjoyed tea made from the engine boiler.'

He's a little boy and he's a man; you can't tell his age any more than a tortoise's. The world has hit him. He's taking it, he's got a good stance, must have been there all the time. How we used to fight, hate each other, refuse to share things, he resenting having to wear out my suits while I had the new ones, he rejecting the opportunities, failing the exams, indifferent to jobs, capricious and wary of any gambits to tame him; me making the most of my luck, my few talents, finding out the short cuts, taking the jobs, playing tennis with the daughter, working when necessary, never looking too hard at anything, sham or lovely. Funny. He with a wife, a nice girl in the snaps he showed me, he with a child, how did it happen to him?

'Did your wife try to put Brylcreem on your hair?'

'No. Nor make a fighter pilot out of me.'

'Does she like you as a private soldier?'

'She doesn't mind me. She might be uppish with you at first. You give that impression.'

'Do I? Ha ha, how bloody funny! Well, I earn five hundred and fifty a month.'

'That's five hundred more than me. I can't get into my trousers with my shoes on.'

'I've got some spare trousers.'

'What? Wear your bloody cast-offs again? No, sir.'

He's different. Sometimes he's the same, just for a flash, but he's changed. Deep deep down he's got some shrapnel in him. He's shy of it. I don't try to find it, but when I look I touch some iron in him with my eyes and I stop looking then. It isn't the thing for one's family to see. Mother would be worried. She'd think it was women, she'd be frightened, she'd be relieved to think it was Burma, the Japs, the limp. It's both. It's an animal, it's terror, it's having killed. I want to take his face in my hands. I suppose that's what women want to do. I wonder what his wound looks like. I won't like it when we're undressing. I used to hate Daddy's wound, the sucked-in holes cratering his thigh. Now he's got it. But Daddy never had any iron in him. That's what was so horrible about Daddy's wounds, because he was so gentle himself.

'Sometimes it's hard to tell which of us is which. It doesn't seem to matter which of us is which. I've never felt that before except with a woman.'

Night comes with its moods indigo, enfolding the streets in its blues. The man with the mongoose and the snakes in wicker baskets, and the man with the monkey, the drum, the patter of villages, both of them vacate their dry perches on the corner, giving way to the tongas, the footsteps, the lorry loads of troops coming in for the night, the brightly lit cafés and clubs, windowless, verandahed, cool. The tableaux of hunger lie grotesque on the sidewalks, the old women under the trees. The colonel shouts for the water-bearer, shouts in vain, rings the bell that won't ring, takes his trousers off and puts them on again. The brothers clean their teeth; under the tap. The women behind drawn curtains powder and paint, considering a wardrobe of gowns. Only the hard-boiled have any tranquillity, know what they are about. The others don't know at all, haven't the faintest idea, are spiritually deserted, emotionally unstable, when they rub their eyes hard there are lights here, there, where, dancing lights beyond closed eyelids. There is such a thing as Nothing. To handle it requires considerable *savoir faire*.

'It's healing all right now. The M.O. in the hospital knows his stuff up there, he used to spend half his time flying to critical operations in Civvy Street. Pity to waste him out here.'

'He's healing you. That isn't a waste.'

'Oh, I don't know. Everything seems a waste out here.'

'You talk great foolishness.'

'I'm thirsty. Shall we have a peg?'

'Water's all right when you're thirsty. Your wound is a nicer one than Daddy's.'

'His was a German one. This is Japanese. They're both pretty nasty. The mark of the beast. If I had a wife, would she like it?''

'It would purify her.'

'You talk like a parson. Put some trousers on and let's eat.'

The tawdry chandeliers suspend their cheap icicles over the frigid assembly. The eyes reconnoitre with the swift thrust and withdrawal of highly trained troops. Never leave your flank unprotected. Feel along the line for the weak point. Use the ground to give you the maximum cover and advantage, always go for the high ground, all's fair in love and war. In a society dominated by the military caste it is proper to make life conform to correct tactical principles. Lots of these boys are new from home. Emergency commissions; very few regulars; surprising how quickly they settle down. Get to know the ropes, join the club as temporary members, get invited to parties, hullo stranger, what have you got to offer? Nothing? But I couldn't. It isn't worth it. I ask you. Is it? Yes, for you maybe. Well, just for you, then. Look, there are those two again. The brothers. Of course the troops don't settle down quite so easily. There are so many of them and so little for them to do. Things weren't intended for them, unfortunately. It's a shame how they get rooked by these hawkers; I'm sure they send some awful trash to their wives; and they can't afford it, I'm sure. I wonder how much they get. How much does a soldier get, George? God, I don't know. Ten rupees a week, something like that. Look at that kid's khaki drill. Like drainpipes. That's what you call issue trousers, isn't it, George? We really must have a couple of them up to Christmas dinner this year. Find two nice ones for me, George, I'd simply love it.

'You don't tell me much about your baby.'

'You don't tell me much about Burma, either.'

'You'll find out about Burma in good time.'

'So will you about a baby.'

'Not much! My leg will be all right in two months. I'll be back before the dry weather comes. I can pull strings. I'll get back to the regiment, before they go in again.'

'Do you want to?'

'What have one's personal wants got to do with it?'

'Pretty well everything. You're daring yourself to go back.'

'Shut up. Don't catechise me.'

'Well, you are. Remember how we were terrified of diving from the Black Rock in Carris Bay and when you'd dived how you used to swagger?'

'It's different now. Look at that woman just coming in. The one in velvet. She's clinical. She's arithmetic. She adds up lots of little sums, calculates other people's interest and lives on it. If there's a difference she takes it away.'

On the troopship the air stank with the bottoms of many lungs, stenches hung over men's feet, the oaths stank of lechery, you couldn't move; when she rolled there was a sick smell. This country has some smells too. In the troop train it was too hard to mind very much, time got lost, there were platforms and beggars and cripples. I wonder whether he'll tell me what happened in Burma. I don't think he will. I'll be off at first light tomorrow, to catch that early train. I hope I wake. Sleeping on a spring mattress between sheets for the first time since I slept with Eunice on embarkation leave, perhaps I'll oversleep. Be on the duff when I get back. Mustn't be on the duff, don't like justice one bit. Mark time, halt, left turn. While on active service returning late from short leave. I wish he'd tell me about Burma.

'Look at those two over there. I know the man. He's a man who hates sleeping by himself. Bad soldiering that. I bet they'll come in late for breakfast and he'll bully the waiter with the big sahib act till he gets some bacon and eggs. I wonder where he met her. She looks rather nice, doesn't she? He's got a loud voice, can you hear him? She doesn't like loud voices. I like that red in her hair.'

'Oh I forgot. Mother said if I met you I was to give you this.'

The boy put a pure white seashell on the table, on the soiled cloth under the bruised flowers, a seashell. His elder brother looked at it, looked at it, looked harder at it than he looked at most things, put his hand out and softly stroked it. 'You must have been very careful with it, not to break it,' he said.

'Mother said if I met you I was to give it to you.'

The elder boy stroked it with his long middle finger, softly caressed it, let his finger stay on it.

'Hallo, Eric. Fancy meeting you here,' a woman's voice broke into his dream, and he jerked himself up and he had a grin on his face.

'Hallo, Pamela,' he said. 'Just fancy. This is my brother. Pamela, Vincent.' The younger boy hardly noticed her at all, because the little seashell was crushed under his brother's finger, it crumbled on the soiled cloth, and he was frightened by it.

He went to sleep as soon as he slid his naked body between the delicious sheets.

Now he is asleep and my thoughts do not harm him, he's oblivious to them now. He isn't offended when I admit that it wasn't real, we didn't really meet, I didn't respond, didn't say with my heart, 'This is my kid brother.' I hope he enjoyed it, I think he did. He wasn't self-conscious of his rough misfitting trousers and shirt any more than of his ungroomed hair. Some gentleness in his nature sees injustices and inequalities as if they were human maladjustments, the tragedy of a bad marriage, not to be condemned. It's comforting when he talks in his sleep, in this vast darkness. It's a warm night, yet there's always this coldness in me, this lurking. Just past the village above Pegu it was quiet, the bamboo copse utterly still, the bodies of Japanese and white men motionless, dead, done with. Violence back in its earth, under the surface, lying doggo, waiting for a step, a jerk, the renewal of itself in movement, a cryptic shot, a puff of smoke, a fool. We will make good the clearing. Orders. Number one section right flanking, number two section fire section. I will go with number one section. I crushed the seashell under my finger. It crumbled. I hardly pressed it at all. I didn't think I'd see him again. When I wake he'll be going. What chance does he stand? What does it mean to *him*?

The clock has chimed twelve, the clock has chimed one, the clock has chimed two. For two hours the stag party has been going on in the room on the right. They've been singing for two hours now. I can't settle down, I can't sleep, life is being wasted in me, going round and round on its empty repetitive journeys, avoiding the encounter, identifying itself with nothing, avoiding love, refusing socialism, rejecting a better world because my self is worse, worse, worse, but doesn't matter, my self doesn't matter, it

175

wasn't because I wanted to, it was bound to be hell, I couldn't, I had to, if only they'd stop singing. It's an hour since they shouted at the manager when he asked them to make less noise, and threw him out with the clatter of tables and the angry sound of feet and fists, calling his skin black, aware of their whiteness, making me worse, worse, worse. It's a jolly good show and I say, I take a dim view of that bloody little chichi trying to turn us out. Kick him in the teeth next time. Aye, aye, aye, I love you ve-e-e-ry much. There'll always be an England. Blue-birds over the cliffs of Dover. Say that everything is still OK dear. I'll be loving you always. Red, white and blue, what does it mean to you? Who could ask for more in sleepy valley?

He could have shot me, but he didn't. All the time I was crossing the clearing he could have got me with his pistol. But he didn't. He waited until I was right by him, till he could make his magnificent thrust. Then he leapt out of the brake and his sword was raised above his head.

So near me I couldn't miss. I've never hit anything with my pistol, except him. It was absurd. Just the reflex action of my trigger finger, before I thought about it, before I screamed. I wish I hadn't screamed.

I'll get up and stop them singing. If I push the narrow door open from the verandah, just one leaf of the door, and switch the light off, the switch is by the door the same as in this room, and kick the table over and get out of the door, I can belt the first one in the teeth as he comes out, I should be able to get away, if I put my tennis shoes on. He'd still be sleeping when I came back. He wouldn't know. It won't disturb him at all...

The fools! They looked at me with their inane grinning faces, in the fug among the fag-ends and the glasses in the ugly room. And I kicked and I hit. My knuckles are burning and wet. It's cold in pyjamas. I'm shivering. Nobody saw me dive into these palms. They're scared of me. They're arguing. They're nothing. I used to think: If they catch me, I'm done for. If they catch me... They... They... But he waited for me with his sword and it was too late. It was simple. And the thing is that you must be the first. Get him first. Otherwise keep away.

What are they doing? Creeping along the verandah... maybe they're going to bash open the door of the lovers... *They've gone into our room*. One with a torch, one with a lathi.

They're beating up my brother. Oh God, oh God, they got him first. He wasn't awake, was he, he wasn't aware of what goes on in the world. Listen, I'm screaming again... I'll kill... I'll kill. Kill now. Kill.

The whole hotel wakes because it is its business, but the world does not wake because another hotel brawl is none of its business and there are plenty of officials and an established procedure for settling that sort of thing, tomorrow and tomorrow and tomorrow.

Afterword

The first thing to say about *In the Green Tree* is that it was not prepared for publication by the man whose work appears in it. When the book was published in February 1949 (though dated 1948), Alun Lewis had been dead five years. The volume was produced by his widow, Gweno, with the help of Gwyn Jones, who is mentioned in the last letter but one. Professor Jones was editor of *The Welsh Review*, where several of Lewis' stories and poems first appeared. Lewis called him 'among editors, my best – because first & most encouraging – mentor'. Jones was also a supporter of Lewis' Caseg Broadsheets, a venture begun in 1941 with the help of John Petts and his partner, fellow-artist and writer, Brenda Chamberlain. Twopenny sheets of illustrated poems by Welsh writers were prepared, whether in English or translated from the Welsh, with the aim of asserting the 'continuity, almost identity, between Wales sixteen centuries ago & Wales today'. It was in a letter to Lewis that Professor Jones incidentally gave the venture its title.

After Lewis' death on March 5, 1944, a selection of his letters appeared in *The Welsh Review*, volume V, no. 2, June 1945. Another selection, by Keidrych Rhys, appeared in *The Times Literary Supplement* in July 1947. Following these, Allen and Unwin, Lewis' publisher, wrote to Professor Jones suggesting the preparation of another volume to follow *Ha! Ha! Among the Trumpets* which would include some letters. An edited version of *The Welsh Review* letters had already appeared in 1946 under the title *Letters from India* from Jones' Penmark Press in Cardiff with a note by Mrs Lewis and preface by Professor A.L. Rowse. These form the core of *In the Green Tree,* together with six stories that Lewis wrote towards the end of his life. The text was prefaced by a 'Sonnet on the Death of Alun Lewis' by Vernon Watkins, which originally appeared in *Wales*, 4, June 1944. Indeed, the collection gains its title from one of the lines of this poem: 'Ah yes, he died in the green/ Tree.' Lewis died aged twenty-eight.

The letters in *In the Green Tree* are all excerpts; no complete letter is included. During editing, many had their wording or punctuation altered; some were spliced together or printed out of chronological order. All of them are written to Lewis' wife or parents and this determines their character: they are introspective but attempt to reassure by sounding conscientious and forward-looking, what Kingsley Amis referred to as 'decent sententiousness'. That they were written by a man who was subject to depression is not in doubt, nor that they reveal him to be alienated both from the world he had left and the one he was adrift in, however stimulating and novel he found it. Repeatedly, he attempts to steady himself and imagines himself working after the war in the progressive causes beloved of his parents. Lewis' earnestness is genuine yet not the whole truth about him nor even the most important part of it. Nor was it untrue; it shows how profoundly influenced he was by the values of the South Walian community he grew up in.

Lewis' letters to his friends, however (alas, most of them unpublished), strike a different note, as when he describes the six poems he wrote at Lake Kharakvasla at Easter, 1943, which express his yearning for the 'ending of the heart and its ache' ('Water Music'). The version given here in letter 15 is more circumspect. Repeatedly, Lewis shades the extent of the disturbance he felt in India, as when he recovered from his football accident in Poona Hospital in January and February 1943 and again at his lakeside camp that Easter and once more in the Nilgiri Hills and Karachi from July to September. His experiences there altered him profoundly but, naturally and inevitably, they are more guardedly expressed here.

In a Postscript to *In the Green Tree*, Gwyn Jones drew attention to the unhappiness he felt had befallen Lewis in India and Burma. The stories, poems and letters from that time are, indeed, disturbed. They reveal how a gifted, sensitive man fell victim to the nihilism within and around him. As the war progressed, he felt the purpose that drew him to enlist in 1940 unravelling, leaving him with the conviction that he was working 'without shape or plot or purpose'. The army seemed to him 'a field of destruction which organizes to destroy' and he himself trapped in a universe of 'things that crumble as they are made and meaningless in history and in the heart'. Such knowledge undid him.

There were, of course, moments of joy, whether in memories of home or the challenge of his strange new environment – jungles, pools, lakes and streams, people. (Images of water play an especially significant part in Lewis' writing.) Nevertheless, they were all coloured by the Forsterian 'ou-boum' or indifference he sensed, an indifference that amounted to despair: as one of his poems from India says, 'creation touching verminous straw beds'.

181

Though Lewis is an exceptionally gifted letter-writer, he himself placed a limit to the value of his own letters. In one of his Indian journals, he writes:

> [My] letters are journaux intimes coloured more than is legitimate with the warmth of the ego when it is speaking to one who, it knows, will receive its words with love.... The poems are even more biased and bigoted. The poet in one sees only a little of it all. Sees what I do not see in daily ways, what I do not talk about when I discuss the future, what I exclude from my hopes for a better world.

His letters are attuned to his humanitarian attitudes; his poetry is more partial and cuts deeper. Lewis liked to quote a line from one of T. E. Lawrence's letters: 'The only minds worth winning are the warm ones about us.' This is the motive that dominates his letters home and that is what makes them warm in turn. The poems and stories, however, are cold.

Why is it that one writer can win our attention by his disclosures of self when another might bore or irritate us? Who can say? With Lewis, we are all attention as he 'feels the world'. His letters are unfailingly responsive and sympathetic. They are unusual in that they do not so much recall as recreate events. Lewis painstakingly rehearses what has happened to him so that he can grasp his experiences imaginatively. A Keatsian specific governs his correspondence, keeping him 'never too far away from the thing' and reliving what has happened to him for his own benefit as much as others'. There are no abstractions or reflections that do not arise naturally from particulars. The letters have a wonderfully organic feel; in them, we see Lewis 'in midstream', never irritably reaching out for fact or reason.

They also afford us valuable insights into his work, like his last poem, 'The Jungle', or 'The Orange Grove'. Lewis always wrote with attractive yet exhausting difficulty. Words often had to be wrenched from him – if, that is, they did not come naturally to him, as the birds to the trees. He was bedevilled by words and had to wrestle with them. And then came the periods of sterility he dreaded.

The short stories included in the volume repeat the theme of an inner spiritual journey to extinction. In reviewing *In the Green Tree* shortly after its appearance, Alun Llywelyn Williams called it 'a chronicle of a pilgrimage, undertaken in search of a fatal secret'. This secret is associated with water, both as an emblem of rebirth and as conclusion, a final throw of the creative dice. The exception to this is 'The Raid', a subtle piece of writing which focuses on an Indian bomber and the soldiers who are sent to arrest him for killing three of their fellows. The writer who brought these contending parties into such a delicate equilibrium was indeed quite out of the ordinary.

Text

Despite their fragmentariness, the letters of *In the Green Tree* are remarkably fluent. Step into them at any one point and they flow as easily as anywhere else. In preparing them for publication here, I have tried to preserve this quality by restoring original punctuation, phrasing and dating and removing all unintentional repetitions. I have separated letters that were joined and restored passages that clarify our understanding of the text. Some minor errors of punctuation or presentation have been silently corrected. Since the publication of *In the Green Tree*, Mrs Lewis has published a fuller collection of her husband's letters as *Alun Lewis Letters to My Wife* (Seren Books, 1989). Wherever possible, I have collated the letters with those and standardised presentation. The stories appear as they did in *In the Green Tree*.

Illustrations

An unusual and distinctive feature of *In the Green Tree* was that it was illustrated by John Petts. There is a frontispiece portrait of the author, done from memory, a title page illustration and twelve engravings placed strategically through the text.

Petts met Lewis in 1941, when he was serving with the Royal Engineers in Longmoor, Hampshire and Petts was a registered pacifist doing agricultural work near Epsom. Petts' engraving of Lewis, done at the time, appeared on the front cover of his first volume of poems, *Raiders' Dawn and Other Poems* (1942). For *In the Green Tree*, he embarked on what he called 'that so difficult thing, a posthumous portrait', and he did so by returning to this engraving. 'I wanted to get, especially, that dreaming quality which spoke of the poet. "Dreaming" is a dangerously "romantic" adjective, by it I mean the lyrical, inturned dwelling on words and their evocation which his expression so often revealed.'

Then, he went on to draw another (though unintentional) portrait of the man in his illustration for 'The Earth is a Syllable':

> somehow, without trying, this head of the wounded officer became very much the head of Alun. His short stories always seem to be his voice speaking anyway [a view Gwyn Jones concurred with; see *Life and Letters To-day*, 36, 67, March 1943]. And this story is Alun entering so very closely into the death of a soldier. Gweno, poor soul, was very distressed when she saw the drawing, and begged me to change it. This, I did to quite a degree, but I can see now that the resemblance shines through (as I feel it should).

The letters that are marked on his forehead ('M 100') show that he is headed for the main dressing station and indicate the time he was injected with morphine. Royal Army Medical Corps men routinely carried ampoules of the drug for use with those who were wounded on active service.

Gweno had had another cause for unhappiness when Gwyn Jones included a paragraph in *Letters from India* describing Lewis' death. This read: 'Whilst preparing to go on patrol before dawn on March 5th, 1944, he was killed accidentally. The last communication from him, probably sent the day before, was a gay birthday greeting.' She wrote to Jones in September 1946 asking him to remove the paragraph at her own expense, if necessary. As it happens, Jones was already under pressure from the War Office to submit a copy of the book for clearance on 'security' grounds and agreed to do so. The question of the subject of Lewis' death was thus avoided.

One of the illustrations Petts prepared struck him as a failure: the one that appears at the end of 'Ward 'O' 3 (b)'. He wanted it to harmonise with Lieutenant Weston's mood as he sits on the ledge of his hospital pool with his hand in the water. This Narcissus-like moment suggests both movement and stillness, peace and danger, and reappears even more powerfully at the conclusion of 'The Orange Grove'. Another image of a hand, one touching a shell, forms the basis for the engraving in 'The Reunion' and was intended to symbolise 'the intrusion of violence and horror and killing, the horror that haunted gentle Alun when, as he wrote, fate and the future "grinned like a Jap..."'

(All quotations from Petts come in a letter to me dated 5 October 1980.)

John Pikoulis

Foreword by Owen Sheers

Owen Sheers is a poet, short story writer and dramatist. Born in Fiji, he was brought up in Abergavenny and educated at Oxford and the University of East Anglia. His publications include *The Blue Book* (2000); *The Dust Diaries* (2004), which won Welsh Book of the Year, and *Skirrid Hill* (2005). He also writes for radio, television and stage.

Afterword by John Pikoulis

John Pikoulis was born in Southern Rhodesia and attended university in Cape Town, Oxford and Leicester. He is Senior Lecturer in English Literature in the Centre for Lifelong Learning at Cardiff University. He is the author of *The Art of William Faulkner* (1982) and *Alun Lewis, A Life* (1984), and edited *Alun Lewis, A Miscellany* (1982). He serves as General Editor of a series of collected works for the Association of Welsh Writing in English, and is co-Chair of the Welsh Academy.

LIBRARY OF WALES

The Library of Wales is a Welsh Assembly Government project designed to ensure that all of the rich and extensive literature of Wales which has been written in English will now be made available to readers in and beyond Wales. Sustaining this wider literary heritage is understood by the Welsh Assembly Government to be a key component in creating and disseminating an ongoing sense of modern Welsh culture and history for the future Wales which is now emerging from contemporary society. Through these texts, until now unavailable or out-of-print or merely forgotten, the Library of Wales will bring back into play the voices and actions of the human experience that has made us, in all our complexity, a Welsh people.

The Library of Wales will include prose as well as poetry, essays as well as fiction, anthologies as well as memoirs, drama as well as journalism. It will complement the names and texts that are already in the public domain and seek to include the best of Welsh writing in English, as well as to showcase what has been unjustly neglected. No boundaries will limit the ambition of the Library of Wales to open up the borders that have denied some of our best writers a presence in a future Wales. The Library of Wales has been created with that Wales in mind: a young country not afraid to remember what it might yet become.

Dai Smith
Raymond Williams Chair in the Cultural History of Wales
University of Wales, Swansea

LIBRARY OF WALES
FUNDED BY

Llywodraeth Cynulliad Cymru
Welsh Assembly Government

CYNGOR LLYFRAU CYMRU
WELSH BOOKS COUNCIL

LIBRARY OF WALES
WRITING FOR THE WORLD

Dannie ABSE

Ash on a Young Man's Sleeve

Ron BERRY

So Long, Hector Bebb

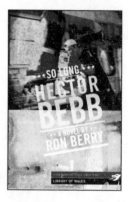

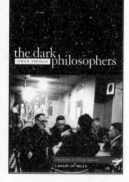

Gwyn THOMAS

The Dark Philosophers

Lewis JONES

Cwmardy & We Live

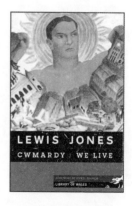

www.libraryofwales.org

Alun LEWIS

In the Green Tree

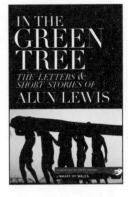

Alun RICHARDS

Home to an Empty House

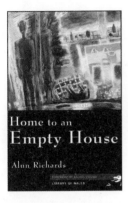

Raymond WILLIAMS

Border Country

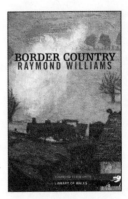

Emyr HUMPHREYS

A Man's Estate

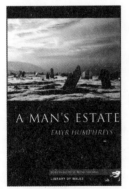

Margiad EVANS

Country Dance

enquiries@libraryofwales.org